HEAR ME OUT

Rox Naval

Ukiyoto Publishing

All global publishing rights are held by

Ukiyoto Publishing

Published in 2022

Content Copyright © Rox Naval
ISBN 9789362699275

All rights reserved.
No part of this publication may be reproduced, transmitted, or stored in a retrieval system, in any form by any means, electronic, mechanical, photocopying, recording or otherwise, without the prior permission of the publisher.

The moral rights of the author have been asserted.

This is a work of fiction. Names, characters, businesses, places, events, locales, and incidents are either the products of the author's imagination or used in a fictitious manner. Any resemblance to actual persons, living or dead, or actual events is purely coincidental.

This book is sold subject to the condition that it shall not by way of trade or otherwise, be lent, resold, hired out or otherwise circulated, without the publisher's prior consent, in any form of binding or cover other than that in which it is published.

Copyediting by The Publishing Consultant
(thepublishingprofessional@gmail.com)
Illustrations by Shiela Rae S. Co

www.ukiyoto.com

*To T, A, H, and C.
This is the dream, Kuya.
This is the dream.*

To T, A, H, and C.
This is the dream, Kuya.
This is the dream.

With much attention to detail, Rox Naval has the reader mingling among a group of off-again, on-again friends who breathe, think, and dream music.

The self-declaratory and intimate perspective of Lu, a young musician who grieves for her deceased brother in ways that she is not even fully aware of, helps the reader to experience how complicated navigating relationships can be, especially for those who are just beginning to understand themselves. The most captivating part is, no surprise, the original lyrics of Naval herself ("Faith, trust, and pixie dust, I've got it all up in my sleeve"), which makes the reader long to hear these words set to music.

This heartbreaking yet hopeful novel is not so much about revelation—truly useful ones happen only after a lifetime—but it is still ascendant. There are more questions than answers among these earnest friends, their relationships sustained by the prospect of music creation, their dedication to artistic expression rising above the mess of entanglements, unexpected departures, and misaligned family expectations.

— Almira Astudillo Gilles, PhD
(author, anthropologist, social scientist, conservationist)

In this debut novel by young writer Rox Naval, a gifted young musician comes to terms with losing a loved one. The story is like a rhapsody that flows from the guitar of our main character, Lucy. Lu's journaling is punctuated by songs of different genres (enriching the reader's knowledge of Gen Z music); each song depicts her raw emotions and unrestrained plaints about life, family, and friendship.

A young reader will surely wonder where all the angst and rage are coming from. The author deftly drops truth bombs at strategic points in the narrative, unfolding and revealing more new stories which could possibly lead to another sequel — perhaps a trilogy?

This is a story that will resonate with many young people who have unexpectedly and prematurely dealt with a loved one's death. Hopefully, Lu's story will help young people move on from their grieving to find light and love in friendship, family, and music.

— Gwenn Galvez
(booktologist)

One of the endearing qualities of this novel is its poignancy. A family tragedy that leads to a rather intense dynamic between Lu and her mother strike out a tune, albeit sharp. But beneath Lu's teenage angst lies the pain of losing a loved one, a backstory that is carefully sprinkled throughout the novel until readers get to the last piece of the jigsaw puzzle. Naval subverts the narrative structure, in such a way that you would think it's over, but it really isn't. Or has the story just begun?

This book is a daring adventure. Jump in if you're brave enough.

— Crissemari Santos
(author, teacher, content creator)

Foreword

Writing a novel at any age is a difficult task and successful young adult novels written by a young adult are few and far between. Therefore, I am always in awe of teenagers who have the perseverance to write long, with clarity, juggle a dozen or so characters, and can tell a good story. Quite an awesome feat!

One of the many gifts of writing fiction is the power to create a world that one wants for herself. This world is clearly set in the Philippines and the consciousness of the characters clearly Filipino even as they speak in English. The novel is sprinkled with expressions like "ay, naku" or "salamat, ate" and parents of friends are respectfully called Tita or Tito. Even the names of the schools are unmistakably Filipino. This is important to note as many young writers, especially those that write in English, model their work on the Western novels they have read.

In her first novel, *Hear Me Out*, Rox Naval creates a familiar yet ideal world that is diverse and inclusive but not without suffering. This is, after all, the human condition. Lu is your typical high school freshman who has mood swings and a bad temper that often alienate her friends and her mother. Lu is burdened by the death of her brother and her mother sends her to summer camp in the hope that Lu can get over Syd's death and the break-up of his rock band. How does one get over a beloved sibling's sudden death? How does anyone heal from a loved one's death? This is always a difficult topic and Rox has accepted the challenge.

In this story of grief and healing, Lu begins her journey of self-discovery, where friendships are questioned and parental authority challenged in an explosion of rock music. Lu's brother Syd loved rock and roll and formed a band that they aptly called Maxxed Out. Lu adopts the remaining band members and Syd's guitar upon his death. But it doesn't work out and Lu is a ball of fury. Forced to attend camp by her mother, she meets old friends, makes new ones and the universe intervenes in many unsuspecting ways. In Rox's capable hands, we witness Lu's transformation made all the more poignant by the music and original compositions that serve as motifs throughout the novel.

The writer is an old soul and both a poet and philosopher. I was charmed by her vegetable philosophy — "For we are all... vegetables! ... Like the vegetables, we're all different. But we're all united under one Bahay Kubo."

I am looking forward to reading more from Rox Naval.

Carla Pacis
Unyon ng mga Manunulat sa Pilipinas (UMPIL)
Lifetime Achievement Awardee
for Children's Literature in English

Acknowledgments

Thank you to those who have helped me become a better writer: Teacher Roel, Mrs. Pascual, Mrs. Henson, Ms. Bagalan, and Tita Gin. I'll continue to hone my writing skills and be more deserving of your commendations. Thank you, Ate Shiela, for bringing Lu and her friends to life through your pretty drawings!

Thank you to my friends, classmates, and family who inspired the characters in this book.

Thank you to my siblings, Kuya Sam, Ate Bel, and Ate D for your tastes in music.

Thank you, Mom and Dad, for supporting me from the very start.

Thank you, TL, Hannah, Avi, and Carrie for helping me get up from my slumps and for being the greatest companions ever.

Special thanks to all the bands I've listened to when I was writing this: The Strokes, Arctic Monkeys, and Stray Kids, to name a few. Your songs definitely comfort teenagers and adults alike.

Lyrics are from these bands: Hall & Oates (You Make My Dreams Come True), 1980; The Strokes (Reptilia, 2003; Someday, 2001); Colony House (You Know It, 2017); IZ*ONE (Fiesta, 2020); and Stray Kids (My Pace, 2018).

Lastly, thank you if you have read this far! May we see each other again in my next book!

Prologue

It was at a friend's party when ninth-grader Syd Garcia saw his friend Ice attempting to smoke. He managed to talk Ice out of it and confiscated the pack of cigarette. As he was about to throw the pack into the trash can, he couldn't keep his eyes off it. It taunted him, made him feel all tingly.

He brought the lit cigarette to his lips and took one big inhale. Quickly, he coughed out the smoke and threw both the pack and the cigarette into the trash.

He never told anyone about this tingly feeling. Not his mom who used up all her energy scolding him after seeing a photo of him with a cigarette from another party. Not even his sister Lu, who was practicing in his room the transition from a G chord to an F chord on a guitar as tall as herself.

"Kuya, could you help me with this chord again?" Lu asked. Syd crawled to her and held her finger.

"Put this finger on this fret," he stretched her finger to where it should be. "Now, apply all your force so the sound will be correct."

Lu noticed something though. "Kuya, why is your hand twitching?"

Syd froze, watching his hand go limp. He let go of Lu's hand and ruffled her hair. "Just tired," he got off his bed. "I'll just grab some water. Put my guitar back, ha?"

"I know."

Syd ran to the kitchen and downed two glasses of water.

Water could be the solution. No one would know about this tingly feeling. They would only assume that he was constantly thirsty. That was okay. He would be okay. Mom would not know. Lu would not know. He could not be a letdown. He could not let Lu down. If Lu knew about his temptation to smoke, she might follow him.

Syd jumped at the sound of Halls and Oates, singing about dreams coming true from his phone. It was a message from Ice.

"Syd! I got Jay to stop smoking! Meet us at the park, we're throwing away all our cigarettes."

In 30 minutes, the three boys stood in front of a trash can in the park.

"You have them, Jay?" Ice's smoky breath infiltrated Syd's nostrils. Jay dumped packs of cigarettes into the trash can.

Syd's breathing was unstable. He placed his hands inside his pockets to stop them from twitching.

Jay looked at Syd, "You told Ice to stop?"

"Yeah."

"You've ever smoked before?"

"Nah," Ice answered for Syd. "He's a kuya. He can't smoke." Syd pursed his lips, his eyes darting from the cigarette packs to them.

"Looks like he wants one," Jay nudged Ice. "Take one then spit it out, if you don't like it." Syd blinked profusely at the offered white and brown stick. Then he started seeing double. Then quadruple. He kept on blinking.

"Syd? Syd?" Ice tried to steady Syd on his toes.

"Water," Syd cracked a smile. Ice tried smiling but fear was written all over his face.

"Sex—" Syd held in a burp. "Drugs—"

"And rock and roll," Ice finished the line for Syd. "I hope you're not going to do something unexplainably stupid."

"Yes, sir—" Syd took deep breaths and lifted his twitching finger. "Burn all those cigs. I got to go."

"Home?" Ice asked.

"The moon, idiot! La Luna!" Syd raised his shaking limbs to the sky before letting them hang loose. He headed home on unsteady feet.

Syd reached home, crawling on all fours up the stairs, stumbling once or twice. Once he reached his room, he rushed to the bathroom and puked. Yet, he still saw two of everything. He reached for the shower knob, twisted it, and out came freezing water from two shower heads.

"God, no, god, no, god—"

Outside his bathroom, his laptop continued to blast The Beatles. The guitar riff of Helter Skelter echoed in his ears. Syd tried to cover his ears, but there was so much noise and movement.

His hands shook violently, his legs wobbled. He took a step back and watched as the room spun around. A loud thud echoed like a gong in his ears, his head stopped spinning, and the floor felt warm underneath. He was on the floor, squinting at the ceiling.

The water from the shower soaked his jeans. Syd saw scenes from his life flashed before him. He saw Lu's face. Then his mom's face. Syd closed his heavy eyes and mumbled words that could have been a prayer.

The heavy riff turned into a mellow acoustic, a fitting lullaby.

"Mom…" he whispered softly. "Please be good to Lu."

I

I gripped the mic, savoring the moment. Screams poured down like waterfalls. There was no beginning, no end. Only a continuous momentum melodiously intertwining with each note. Something about the screams was comforting, satisfactory. I waved at them, the desolate crowd. My tan hands were the only things that I focused on. The weight of the Fender guitar became heavy. I was able to catch its neck before it fell completely onto the stage. The wooden platform I stood on... Was I with someone else? That did not matter. I continued to wave at the void, looking up, and then down at my shoes. This is the dream, Kuya. I did it. I did —

"Why don't you want to join this camp?"

Mom's voice snapped me out of my daydream. Camp? This was the fifth camp I asked Mom to decline.

She continued, "How else are you going to get better?"

Damn. "I told you I don't want to pursue mathematics," I repeated. "Is it that hard to understand? I want to do music."

She pouted at me.

"Lucy," she said in that sing-song Mom tone. That damned tone. She's going to ask me if music is my passion or if I'm just doing it for Syd.

"Are you sure you aren't forcing music into your life?" See? "You want to become a math teacher, don't you? You've been so adamant about it ever since you were five."

Freaking shit, enough with the past aspirations, Mom! I sighed. "Mom, just don't let me go to that camp." I did not want to fight with her. It would've been the seventh time this week.

"Lucy," her tone changed. My eyes rolled at her sternness. "I hope that by the time school starts, you snap out of your music phase. Syd would've wanted you to continue focusing on Math because you're so good at it." She ended her litany with a smile as if it would snap me out of my so-called phase in an instant.

It was as if she expected me to say, "Oh! Music wasn't made for me! You're so right mom! You're so damn right! Syd wouldn't want me to continue music! I mean, why else would he have offered me to join him in forming Maxxed Out?"

"Lucy?" My mom called me back to Earth. I looked at her tired eyes then back down at my shoes. "Okay?"

Oh, how those brown eyes irritated me so much.

"Fine," I mumbled my way out. Not even looking back at her droopy face, I left her sighing as I walked up to my room. I heard her slam the door to her office. I clenched my fists.

Why the hell did Kuya say Mom and I would be the best duo? Mom had baduy ideas. She would have preferred a crappy 9–5 job for me as long as it meant I was not touching a guitar. It was different with Kuya. Whenever Syd was around, she was ecstatic about Maxxed Out, about me, him, and two other kids playing instruments and singing for fun. Man, she would go everywhere telling all the titos and titas about our band as if we already released bestsellers.

When Syd died almost four years ago and those two kids left, Mom suddenly went from 'music is so great' to 'music killed my son.' Zero idea where she picked up this mindset. Syd would never have blamed his death on music. Never. But Mom went a full 180 the moment he died.

I hated her for that.

I slid my door closed as I walked toward my phone that rested on top of my black guitar bag. I held the pudding keychain and unzipped the black bag to reveal a red Fender guitar that belonged to Syd. I brought it out and rested it on my black denim jeans. Opening the front pocket where all the odds and ends were, I felt for my guitar pick. I pulled out a four-year old birthday card instead. It was dated December 10. Two months after, he died.

Dear Lu,

Happy birthday!
Believe in Mom more.
You two are the best duo out there!

Love,
Syd

I stared at Syd's messy writing while I rubbed the rough guitar pick in between my middle and pointer finger. My phone began to vibrate, startling me.

What I want, you've got.
And it might be hard to handle.
But like a flame that bu—

I clicked decline to stop the song from playing. I wasn't sure if I still wanted to hear Hall and Oates' You Make My Dreams whenever someone calls, but this was Syd's ringtone and I was just so used to hearing this. I scrolled through the notifications on my phone.

3:05 pm. Five missed calls. Twenty new messages from Maxxed Out. One new message from Emmie two hours ago: "Do we still have band practice at 3?"

"Crap."

I stuffed the card inside the front pocket and shoved the guitar back, yanking the pudding keychain to zip it up. I checked the metal hook that held the pudding to the chain, hoping I did not yank too hard. Feeling assured that the pudding keychain was still intact, I hauled the case over my shoulder, but stopped in my tracks before sliding the door open.

I knew that after every confrontation, Mom went to her office and watched television before going up to her room to sleep. If I opened the big main door leading downstairs then I knew she would be suspicious of me walking out with my guitar case. I thought of the riskiest thing to do.

I grabbed a bunch of clothes, cushioned my guitar, and opened the window facing the house across ours. My fingers felt ticklish as I leaned forward. The patterned beat of Mom's footsteps going up the stairs was getting louder. I had to jump quickly.

I took a deep breath and whispered what Syd taught me a long time ago before you do something stupid.

"Sex, drugs, rock 'n' roll."

With that, I twisted the guitar and held it tight against my chest before leaping out the window and landing on my right side. I sneaked down the gravel road and ran out the gates to the village clubhouse, unaware of the gash in my upper arm that was slightly bleeding.

2

It was 3:10 in the afternoon when I reached the clubhouse. Everyone seemed comfortable in the rented room while waiting for me. They were facing the mirrored wall that occupied one whole length of the room.

Sachiko was sitting on one of the white foldable chairs, her back straight, and her eyes glued to her phone screen. I heard sugoi as her fingers tapped like machines on high speed. Her keyboards are nicely set up in one corner.

Emmie held her phone in the same position as Sachiko, but was too immersed in watching Sachiko's screen. Leaning against Emmie's chair was a black guitar bag that held her bass she named Brian for the fun of it.

Alex leaned against the smooth wooden wall while talking to someone on her phone. She was probably saying: "Two pizzas please. One with pepperoni and one with cheese, please. Sampaguita clubhouse. Salamat po."

Lastly, there was thoughtful Maya who, once she saw me, ran around her drums and toward me, embracing me tightly. I yelped. The moment I let a sound out from my mouth, she stopped in an instant and took off my flannel to reveal the wound.

"Lu, what happened?!" She asked, evident concern on her face. The other three rushed toward us to join the action.

I shrugged and replied, "Sex, drugs, rock 'n' roll." Syd told me the phrase was also used to escape telling anyone about the stupid stunt you did that would concern them.

Maya let go, sighed, and rummaged through her canvas bag to bring out a pink pouch full of bandages and medicine. We called it the first-aid-kit-that-exists-because-of-someone-named-Lu. After taping a small gauze pad on my arm, I placed my flannel back on and brought my guitar bag to the front to unpack.

I looked at everyone, who were already used to my antics that they didn't move an inch from their place.

Maya was always the artsy type, yet she never could let things go quite easily. So sentimental. Her bag was an eighth-grade antique with distinct button pins scattered all over the front. I could tell who gave which. Sachiko gave the majority of the cat pins. Alex's bun dance pin was right next to Emmie's drum set pin. The country pins were from her sister Mika who placed it there against her will while my Arctic Monkeys pin remained in its place at the center. It was the only black pin on her bag, I felt very proud that it stood out.

Peeking out her of bag were magazines one would see at a hair salon, plus a few hair accessories — clips, pins, barrettes. If our school actually allowed her, she would have a handful of colored pins up in her hair. It's the only thing she could do for now because her mom was pretty protective of Maya's long and wavy locks.

"Let's start na." I placed the strap of the Fender over my head. Everyone casually brought their instruments to position. Since we rented the room, Sachiko and Maya prepared their instruments ahead of time. It seemed less of a hassle to do instead of hauling it around like the rest of us. I plugged the wire attached to my guitar into a small amp that Alex brought from her house, strummed my fingers against the strings. Satisfied.

"Ready?" I looked at myself in the mirror. It was a thrill to be in front. I was the smallest in class so I was accustomed to it. I grew to like it.

"Yeah," Sachiko turned her keyboard on and quickly played Twinkle, Twinkle Little Star to warm up. Alex strongly strummed her guitar, emitting a loud metal-like sound from her amp. Emmie plucked each thick string of her bass before mumbling, "Yep."

"Let's do Reptilia," I positioned my fingers for the first chord. "Maya?"

Maya lifted her sticks up high and chanted with every whack. "One, two, one, two, three, go!" We played our instruments, following Maya's beat.

He seemed impressed by the way you came in...

I kept the low voice constant, closing my eyes to listen carefully to each individual instrument.

Alex's fingers moved swiftly as she jumped from chord to chord, from bar to bar, they were racing cars moving here and there at max speed while still keeping to the beat of Maya's drum. If Alex's fingers were the hare, Emmie's fingers were the turtle, stable and focused, not planning on going wild anytime soon.

Sachiko's keyboards gave a rather modern feel to the band. The little melodies she added by pressing her fingers onto the white and black keys.

Maya's beats remained strong throughout the song, like the pied piper luring the children out of Hamelin.

My voice stayed calm like a car on the flat road, enjoying the breeze from the ocean it drove past. The first verse went by so easily with no mistakes.

If I was given a peso for every lie I've said, I would have six pesos. We sounded like shit and we knew it.

At the last strum, there was a knock on the door.

"I'll go get it!" Sachiko jogged to the door while turning on her phone. A second later, there was a loud thud that startled everyone. She dropped her phone.

"Uh...I came to deliver pizza?" The delivery boy looked concerned, slowly inching his box of pizza toward the frozen Sachiko.

Alex entered their space and accepted the box of pizza while looking intensely at the boy. She glared at those who seemed like possible threats to Sachiko. Once you receive one of Alex's glares, you're fucked. Seriously.

The boy nodded to brush off Alex's glare. He bent down and retrieved Sachiko's phone with its lavender case and anime girl keychain that jingled and jangled. Holding only the end of the phone with one hand and his other hand holding its wrist, he waited for Sachiko to get the phone from him. Swiftly, Sachiko swiped the phone from the boy's hand and ran far away from the door. A gust of wind hit me as she ran past me. We waited for the twinkle of her game to play before turning our attention back to the pizza boy.

"That'll be 298 pesos," he said as Alex rummaged through her pockets. I felt my heart race, I knew that voice.

"Lu! Do you have 98 pesos?" Alex shouted from the door. I sighed, removed the strap, and let my guitar rest on the guitar bag. Rummaging through the pockets of my jeans, I was able to pull out an extra 100 peso bill my mom gave me last week. I rushed up to Alex and passed her the bill, and tried to avoid looking at the delivery boy. I watched her flatten out the crumpled bill and hand it over to the terrifyingly tall boy, but I had to look.

"Lu?" He wore the same shocked expression as mine. "I got a bit of nostalgia when she said your name," he spoke out. "How's missing math—"

"Thanks for the pizza. Alex let's go," I did not bother listening to him and grabbed Alex's arm and dragged her away from the door, slamming it behind us.

"Who was that?" Alex checked if he was still there.

"Yeah, who was he?" Sachiko mumbled, hoping the music from her game would be louder than her voice.

Emmie rolled her eyes. "Boys ain't worth shit. They're stupid anyway."

"I do think boys are okay," Maya politely inserted herself in the conversation, "but we don't need them to survive." Emmie nodded, giving me a weird look and not thinking twice before blurting.

"Lu looks like the type who wouldn't be into bo—"

"His name is Aerol."

I stopped the conversation from going anywhere else. I slouched and grabbed a slice of pizza. "He used to be in that band with me and Syd."

"Ahhhh..." they chorused at the mention of my brother. It was a sensitive topic, so we avoided it as much as possible. We proceeded to shove the pizzas down our throats. I smiled as Alex ate two pizza slices at once like a sandwich.

Emmie looked out the window, the sky showcased a blue-orange gradient. "Sach, what time is it?" Her face lit up as Sachiko paused her game to check the time.

"4. 5. 2." Sachiko read the numbers on her phone. The band took a minute to process what she meant.

"Ah," we all realized she meant 4:52.

Sachiko moved to Manila just last year, and she already mastered a lot of English words for someone who had been living in Japan most of her life. She still had trouble reading numbers and understanding quick conversations, but if it was about her game, she was the most talkative. Other than that, she rarely talked.

I knew what came next and rolled my eyes at Emmie's lil' smile that showed off her bunny teeth. "Lu, it's close to five."

"Yeah, we should get going," Alex joined Emmie, stacking the pizza boxes and placing the napkins inside them.

"We literally practiced one song," I tried to snap them out of laziness. "Just one more," I pleaded.

"But, Lu!" Emmie whined, "It's so late!"

"We have school the next day, Lu," Sachiko inserted herself at the wrong time. "We have to prepare."

"There'll be traffic, too," Maya pouted. I sighed in disbelief at my band. Once one gets lazy, everyone is infected.

"Besides, your mom might freak out," Emmie pointed to her arm. "Best to go home early so you can wash the bloodstain off your red flannel." She smiled. I rubbed my eyes in utter annoyance. I could not convince them to stay as long as I liked because we had secrets to keep from our mothers. We all told them we had a study session that ended at six, but we could not even go beyond five as everyone wanted to leave at the sight of the orange-blue sky. Emmie did have a point with my arm, sort of.

I sighed and stood up, "Good practice everyone. Let's clean up and get out of here." Everyone cheered as they packed up their instruments and threw away the pizza boxes and tissues. Emmie, Alex, and I hauled our guitar bags over our shoulders while Maya held her drumsticks and Sachiko brought all her focus back on her phone.

"Those drumsticks must be heavy," Alex sarcastically commented.

"Yeah, they weigh a ton," Maya played along, making Alex laugh. She then noticed the small pudding keychain that dangled from my guitar bag.

"Lu," Maya played with the pudding keychain, "you're not the type to have this cute keychain."

"Oh, that." I sounded really embarrassed. I was. Pudding keychains were something Maya would have. Heck, if she had a guitar bag, it would be full of all these keychains that were either borderline cute or borderline creepy. I did not want the keychain to be the center of attention, so I looked up at the now orange sky and recalled what day it was.

"Last day of summer, huh?" I heard everyone hum in agreement.

"I wasted my summer playing drums," Maya used her index and thumb to spin her drumstick, "but I wasted it with the four of you so it wasn't so bad."

"You didn't just play the drums," Alex stretched her arms. "You ate, drank, binged TV, ate, drank, slept… did I mention you ate—" She yelped, feeling Maya's drumstick poke her stomach. Emmie covered her mouth, trying not to laugh in front of the crouching guitarist. Making fun of Maya is kind of like bringing a boy up to your room to hang out when your mom is in the house, it's not the best thing to do if you want to keep your body intact.

"How will Sachiko keep up with all the big words the English teacher might give?" Maya glanced at Sachiko, whose upper torso was in her own world while her legs were on Earth.

"She'll survive," Emmie replied coolly, "I mean if she was able to use 'metaphorically' in a normal conversation, she'll survive high school literature."

"Since when did Sachiko use that word?" I asked in disbelief. It's not every day that a kid who's told to speak another language ends up using a word meant for essays.

"When she was playing her game once during practice and Alex was trying to tap her screen to make her lose points," Emmie explained.

Maya nodded, "I remember."

Emmie continued, "Maya was reading some playscript her mom told her to read. And she read out loud: headless, metaphorically, brainless… I don't know basta it was some poetic kind of junk and that crap makes me braindead, but anyways —"

Maya took over, "Alex told Sachiko: Hah! A chair can play better than you."

Emmie resumed the story, "Sachiko overheard me reading out loud at that moment, paused her game, and glared at Alex saying—"

"Metaphorically, I would throw a chair on you and watch you bleed to death," Alex finished the story, looking at the road that lies far ahead of her as if reminiscing. "That was probably the darkest and most literate thing Sachiko has said so far."

"And I would say it again," Sachiko's interruption scared all of us. The moment she finished, a high pitched "nice job!" came from her phone. She raised her hand into a small fist and whispered "Yes!"

"Wait. When did this happen?" I was dumbfounded. We spent nearly the whole of July together and not once have I encountered any of Alex pestering Sachiko, or heard Maya's script. They were very calm when they told me the answer.

"While you were up front playing your guitar," Alex did a horrible impersonation of an air guitar.

Man, all this happened without me knowing. Brushing it off, I looked at my feet as we walked on the gravel road, listening to my friends' chatters at the back and Sachiko's never-ending full combos. I was clueless.

I thought of freshman year. The movies prepared us for this shit. The idea of high school made me overthink about many things, mostly issues based on the rom-coms Syd watched. Do they have jocks? Are the teachers actually homework maniacs? How will we use the lockers? Will the boys be assholes? But the most important question was probably how to survive the opening ceremony tomorrow.

Mr. Reyes, our music teacher, personally sent me an email a few days before July as he was the person who introduced Alex to us when we were just starting as a band. He requested us to perform at the opening ceremony

"Aren't we playing for the opening ceremony tomorrow?" Maya's sudden realization drew groans from everyone.

"Is that old fart serious?" Alex looked pissed, slouching as she walked with her guitar resting on her back.

"Ugghhh," Emmie's groan was loud. "I don't want to do this stupid ceremony. Can we have someone else do it?"

"Fudge, no!" I objected. Everyone stiffened. "We're a band, remember? This can be our first step to greatness." I turned around and steadily walked backward so I could focus on them.

"If we declined, then a month's worth of practice would go to waste, right?" They all sighed and nodded in agreement.

"Lu's right," Maya smiled, hoping it could comfort me.

"Come on," I tried to lighten the mood, "The audience will be amazed at how awesome Maxxed Out is." I smiled, visualizing the screams and applause from scary high schoolers.

This will become our starting point. This is where the story starts. The story of five friends, on a journey to greatness. Everyone will remember their name as the greatest band alive. They'll chant until their voice boxes grow sore. Maxxed Out! Maxxed Out! Maxxed Out!

"Bye, Lu," Emmie's goodbye brought me back to Earth. Suddenly, everyone was going their own separate ways. I felt my face burn, realizing I was in front of my house, too busy thinking about tomorrow to focus on what was happening now.

"See ya, chibi!" Alex waved, laughing at her new nickname for me.

"See you tomorrow, Lu!" Maya waved, nudging Sachiko to say bye to me.

"Bye," Sachiko mumbled.

Maya laughed nervously before turning around to walk Sachiko back to their village. They were neighbors so they always walked home together.

There was silence before I waved back, "See you all tomorrow..."

By the time I said goodbye, everyone was gone. I sighed, entered the back door to avoid my mom giving me her I-know-you-sneaked-out look, and to come up with another dumb excuse.

3

I opened the door, tensing up as it creaked softly. The living room was empty. I sighed happily, relaxing my muscles as I brought the guitar bag inside.

"Mmm," my mom hummed in a low tone that made me jump and almost cussed.

"Mom, I ah—" I gulped, adjusting the strap on my shoulder, "You're up."

She wasn't buying it, "Where did you go with that guitar?"

"Oh, wow, someone knows her instruments," I praised her. "RJ's music store down the street." My brain wrote a whole story at max speed, trying to think of today's fake plot.

"And what did they say?"

They did not want the guitar because it was too old. No, no. She might go there directly. They were closed? But you just told her you went there. The dumbest idea entered my head.

"There was a fight at the store and they didn't allow kids to be at the place of violence." I looked at my mom, I was tensed, waiting to find out if I passed the first round of auditions at The Voice.

My mom's eyes widened, "A fight?"

Oh, dear. "I'll tell you about it at dinner." I walked past her, taking off my shoes and bringing them upstairs. "I'll go shower!" I shouted, letting the huge wooden door that separated the kitchen from the living room close by itself as I headed to my room.

Outside it was warm, but my room seemed warmer. I sweated in my flannel. Flinching, I slowly took off the red flannel and removed the white cloth Maya placed on the wound. I extended my arm, tolerating the sting the wound gave as it stretched.

> *A red crate on the planet*
> *Red like plump lips*
> *Red like the human heart, forever beating on and on*
> *On and on*
> *But can it beat for another?*
> *Red like a candle stamp on an envelope*
> *shielding words of sadness, anguish*
> *or did it hide words of happiness, missing?*
> *whatever the letter had, it can never be delivered*
> *Forever stuck to my hands, I'm afraid to give it to you*
> *You, who is not in front of me.*

I shook my head. Stupid words. I opened my guitar bag and placed the guitar on its stand before grabbing the nearest black shirt and gray shorts, stuffing the rolled-up underwear in my pocket before speedwalking to the bathroom.

Of course, Mom had to open the big door when I was right smack in the center of the common room. We locked eyes before she screamed at my wound.

"Lu, what happened?" She was going for my arm. I backed up before she could touch me.

"Ahh... I really wanted to give back this guitar but oh, stubborn me!" I nervously laughed, hoping my mom would laugh back.

"Lu, take a shower then apply Betadine on your arm," she ordered me. "Next time I'll be the one to give the guitar back to RJ."

My smile faded. I avoided her eyes. I hated looking at those brown eyes.

She sighed heavily, walking away from me and closing the door to her own room. I was alone once again, satisfied at the sound of everything but her voice. I exhaled in content, walking to the bathroom to shower.

The small room echoed the guitars of the Strokes. Julian Casablancas' voice bounced off the walls. I closed my eyes, memorizing the position of the chords and the strumming pattern as warm water poured on my face. I tilted my head back, instantly regretting it once I felt drops enter my nostrils. Instantly, I turned off the shower to stabilize my breathing, while Julian Casablancas sang, unbothered.

> *And now my fears, they come to me in threes. So, I sometimes...*
> *Say, fate, my friend, you say the strangest things, I find, sometimes...*

I sang along as I showered. With a deep breath, I closed my eyes tightly as the warm water poured on my body. I stepped out, grabbed my towel, and stayed still. Take this moment to relax, I told myself. It would be hell from here on out.

♪♪

I rushed down to the smell of kaldereta from downstairs. My hair was dripping, making the fabric on my shoulders a shade darker than the rest of the shirt. I sat across my mom, scooping myself a big spoonful of rice, letting a few grains fall off. I smothered the kaldereta sauce over the rice before placing the beef on top. My mom watched me in silence before speaking up.

"You eat like your brother," she meant it in an endearing way. I swallowed the food in my mouth before smiling back at her, a bit shy to admit that Syd's habits have gotten to me. She fed herself a spoonful of rice and beef before speaking again, "Are you ready for school tomorrow?"

"Mmmhhh," I hummed, too busy chewing the glorious kaldereta.

"Don't bring your guitar tomorrow," my mom was preparing another bite for herself. I dropped my spoon, staring at my food. I remained silent, waiting for her to continue. "I'm bringing the guitar back to RJ, right?"

I kept my eyes on my plate, good enough for one last spoonful. "Don't!" I objected almost immediately. She looked at me like she was questioning my sanity.

"And why is that?" She placed her spoon down and leaned back, waiting for another dumb excuse to escape my mouth.

"I ah—" I was too busy cursing at my brain for not thinking when I needed it to, "Ahh....ah! I've got music class tomorrow! Yeah, Mr. Reyes needs me to bring my guitar so I can perf—ahh...demonstrate for class."

I held onto the hem of my shirt, praying that was a good enough reason. I mean, I wasn't really lying. Mr. Reyes really needed the guitar. My mom did not look convinced, but she did nod and pushed the remaining rice onto her spoon using her fork.

"Okay but you need to get rid of that guitar," she looked at me dead in the eye, pointing her fork at me, "Or you're never going to move on."

I felt a punch in my gut at the overused point my mom had been making to convince me to get rid of Syd's guitar. I lowered my head, finishing my last spoonful of food before wiping my mouth and walking to the kitchen with my empty plate. I came back with a small cup of ice cream to calm my emotions. My mom still had more to say as she did not stand up from her spot.

"Aerol is inviting you to another one of Tita Xandra's camps." I looked away, closing my eyes tight at the feeling of Antarctica in my mouth and at the vision of another boring camp with Aerol.

"Sige na, Lu! Aerol is going to this Bayanihan camp! It has a good Math program. You might be interested. You'll be excused din from school. Isn't that great?" I could not relate to Mom's energy.

I sighed, "Just tell Tita I have cla—"

"I already signed the reply slip."

I slammed my cup on the table, and stood up at my mom's calm reply. "Why did you do that?" I was on the verge of screaming. My heart was beating too fast and my ears were ringing from the thumps it made.

"Because you'll be away from your noise and be one with nature," she smiled, unaware of my suffering.

"Plus, you'll be excused from school for this certain camp. Don't you want that?"

Well, two weeks away from my mom sounded lovely, I thought about it, but at the cost of parting with my guitar?

"I'll give it some thought," I grabbed the half-finished cup of ice cream and continued to feel the leafy taste of matcha melt in my mouth. She sighed.

"Don't bail out on this, ha?" She was so adamant about it as she stood up to put her own dishes in the sink. "This can be good for you so you can make new friends."

I shot back. "But I'm okay with my current friends."

She looked at me and used her helpless tone. "What I'm saying is that maybe, you're hanging out too much with Emmie and Maya that you might lose your connections with Aerol and Dani." She put on her helpless tone of voice. The tone she would use when she just wanted me to straight away agree with whatever bullshit she had up her sleeve.

My fist tightened at the last two names. We should make that a curse word, I thought to myself to lighten up, the 'd' word and the 'a' word. Both words could send an innocent soul to jail.

"I said I'm fine with my current friends," I closed the lid of the ice cream cup. "Dani and Aerol can both burn in hell."

"Hey!"

Oh, crap! I said something bad! Only this time, I meant it! "Sorry."

"I don't see you three hanging out anymore. That's all," she sat down. "No need to be mad at me."

If I could just hit you with a chair metaphorically, I would.

"Ahhh, is that so?" I tried to push all my anger down my body so I would not sound annoyed. It takes practice but I would not say I nailed it. "Well, just an FYI, I did talk to Aerol today." I sounded proud of it. Anything to get my mom thinking that I was handling life pretty well.

"Okay."

"May I be excused?" I inhaled. My mom nodded. I did not even bother looking at my mom's face before marching upstairs and isolating myself in my room.

The heat was unbearable, but sitting in front of my mom talking about simpler times was way worse. I wrapped my hand around the guitar's neck and lifted it from the stand. I positioned the guitar so it laid comfortably on my thighs. Fixing my fingers on the frets, I slowly closed my eyes. I saw Syd, soaked in his puddle of blood as water from the faucet dripped endlessly. I opened them almost automatically. I pushed the guitar upward so I could hug its body tightly. Closing my eyes tight and breathing slowly, I rested my chin on its smooth brown wood, wrapping my arms around it like a boa snake.

I still had Maxxed Out. I still had Syd.

I was not most kids. Once they entered the school building, they would immediately take a right turn and head over to McDonald's or anywhere that wasn't the sanctuary of adults telling you crap about the mitochondria, probably pulling off some Ferris Bueller's Day Off trick. I would have done the same if I wasn't raised in an Asian household.

My mind was still in a daze by the time my shiny school shoes hit the concrete school grounds. When Syd was still in school, I observed his demeanor around his friends when I got the chance to. I was pretty lucky because I always waited for him at the bistro across the parking lot, where most students went to chat and to wreak havoc. I also observed how he would walk toward the high school building. My naive ass thought I would settle in quickly if I acted the same way my brother did.

Here goes nothing. I slowly took in a chunk of air and exhaled it out. The Strokes still blasting loud as ever through my earphones, I speedwalked past two empty bistros. All the students had probably gone up 30 minutes ago. The dean of students was too busy reprimanding two middle schoolers to notice me walking past him. Checking my phone for the title of the playing song, I adjusted my guitar bag that wobbled with every step I took and groaned silently as I climbed up two more flights of stairs.

My school has two main buildings, one for high school and another for elementary. I've stayed in the elementary building for so long that the high school building had looked horrifying. It was a scary place for an eight-year-old who watched her older brother waved and speedwalked his way into the building.

Entering the building felt like entering hell. It was a thought that I dreaded the most. Whenever Syd took a bit too long to reach the bistro, it would mean that he was hanging out with his friends and that I had to enter the high school building to look for him. Most times, I would stay near the library's entrance across from the high school entrance, and I would stay there thinking if I used telepathy then Syd would come down immediately. I wanted to stay away from that building of puberty and nasty teenagers as much as possible.

As years passed, I became one of these nasty teenagers.

The hallway looked like a tiangge during a holiday rush, or a pigsty from the movie Spirited Away. I had zero idea why I felt my stomach hit rock bottom. There were teenagers who looked like iron giants from my perspective. The seniors, juniors, and sophomores loomed over me. Not even the loud guitar solos in the music I was listening to could calm my uneasy breathing. I could see my brother's friends from the ends of the lockers, laughing as if Syd never existed. I held the hems of my jacket. My legs were unable to move at the sight of these older kids looming over me.

Moths were fluttering in my stomach — the kind you would see hovering over a flickering lightbulb at the center of an empty ceiling — and stuck on the sides of my insides, zooming right and left as older kids walked past me. Their uninterested gazes were looking through me.

"Welcome to high school, Lu!" I wished I had Syd tell me, "Most people here are dicks but let me introduce you to the ones that are tolerable." I bit my lip.

Looking at the empty staircase, then at the clock that read 7:20 a.m., I still got 15 more minutes to kill before I'm considered late. I could walk the other way and walk out the gates if the guards did not catch me. I could take a right and head over to McDonald's nearby, grab a 10-piece chicken nugget meal with cola, and jog to the open market a few blocks away.

"No," I grumbled. "Mom's going to get mad at you." It was my way of telling myself to not do something.

Cursing reality, I held onto the straps of my black backpack and marched my way to the lockers. Automatically, I looked for the locker with my class number and twisted the padlock to input the code the school gave me. I can't really explain how I memorized these numbers. The dean of students just gave them to me and boom! 35, 23, and 21 became numbers that stood out to me. Hearing the padlock click, I shoved my school bag inside along with my lunch box and grabbed a few books before inserting the padlock back again.

The stinging smell of Victoria Secret perfume exploded in my face like morning breath, infiltrating my nostrils, and itching my throat. The girls in my class carried cologne like pepper spray. But it was quite lively to see smiles from classmates who had not seen each other since May. I spotted the teacher's desk not far from where I stood. Licking my lips, I searched for the two pieces of paper that were stuffed into my guitar bag. Pulling them out, I read each of them as I faced the small trash can directly underneath the big aircon.

One was a birthday card and another was a reply slip. Nothing but bullshit written on them.

> *I allow my child, Lucy Garcia, to attend this two-week program.*

Syd's messy cursive echoed Mom's medical prescription writing. His writing slanted downward then would rise back up only to drop down again, looking like a zigzag of a sentence. Mom's writing looked no different from her signature. I could only spell out my name because there were only two letters in between the spaces.

"Bullshit," I muttered under my breath. As if the camp could bring about a miracle.

"Lu!" I turned toward the silvery and spirited voice.

"Sachiko," I stuffed the reply slip into my pocket, letting my two fingers hold onto the birthday card.

"You still have your brother's birthday card?" Sachiko bent down to observe the vibrant card. "That's so sweet!"

"Ah, yeah." I gave it one last look before placing it back into the front pocket of my guitar case, "You happen to know where I'm sitting?"

"Next to me," Sachiko smiled, grabbed my wrist and dragged me to the back of the classroom near Emmie and Alex. Maya walked toward us with a frown.

"The teacher placed me in front," she pretended to cry dramatically. "It was a fun seven years at the back of the classroom with you, guys."

"Man, that sucks," Alex shrugged from her seat. She sat one row in front of me and Sachiko, closest to the window that showed you the hallways where the dean was always making everyone aware that she was present with her annoyingly loud heels.

"Yeah," Emmie patted the corner of my table then shrugged at Maya. She sat two seats away from Alex, so she would just have to twist around to speak to me. "Looks like you'll have to say goodbye to free math answers."

"Nooooo!" Maya rested her head on my table. "This has to be the worst school year ever."

"The school year hasn't even started!" Sachiko pointed out.

"Exactly," Maya gave her a no-shit-Sherlock look. Despite being able to use metaphorically in a threat, Sachiko did have trouble telling when Maya was being too dramatic or actually being serious. It was a skill that could not be acquired overnight.

I slid onto my seat, hauling my big guitar bag next to my chair. Holding on to Mr. Pudding to unzip the case, I searched for everyone else's instruments, "Is everyone ready for later?"

"Really wish Mr. Reyes gets a concussion and forgets we had to perform today," Alex buried her face into her arms.

"Hey, we'll do great," Maya rubbed Alex's back. "We did spend the whole summer practicing. I think the performance will go well."

"Plus, it's bad to wish Mr. Reyes gets a concussion," Emmie brought out a small bag of Doritos from under her hoodie. "Placing laxatives in his coffee and locking the boy's bathroom sound like a safer move."

A shittier one though.

"Well, whether or not you like it," I brought out the guitar out of my bag, strumming its strings, "We are playing on that stage. The five of us. It'll be great, trust me."

"Garcia, put your guitar in our designated instrument corner."

The voice came from a rather young lady who entered the room and pointed at the corner of the room where everyone else's guitar bags were found. She looked like she only slept for six minutes instead of her desired seven hours. Glancing at everyone nervously, I brushed my short hair back, letting it return to its original spot near my eyes as I walked to the corner. One hand held the neck of my guitar while the other held my guitar bag.

"While she's doing that," the teacher kept her eyes on me like a hawk, calling the attention of the girls who joined in the staring contest, "There will be an opening ceremony at the gym later."

Murmurs were heard throughout the class.

"I don't know who the band is, but it's a band that Mr. Reyes was very excited to showcase."

"It's my band, Miss!" I turned around, raising my hand despite standing. All eyes on me once again, but it did not bother me. I was about to show the school what my band has up our sleeves.

"Your band?" The teacher kept her eyes on me before looking at the guitar bags at the back. "Oh, so those are not for music class?"

"No, Miss," I comfortably slid in my seat. "Mr. Reyes emailed us, start of the summer to practice."

"What's the name of your band?" The teacher mumbled, too busy texting the other teachers on her phone to care about our band's name.

"Maxxed Out!" I said proudly. Some kids turned around to look at me in disbelief. Some of my classmates had siblings who were classmates with Syd.

"That band still exists?" Pat, the volleyball captain, blurted out of curiosity. "Even after Syd—"

"Dude!" Her friend Ari screamed. Pat covered her mouth as she responded to the glares she was receiving. The teacher gave me a confused look. I fiddled with my fingers, feeling my palms grow sweaty.

"Oh, umm, well, it was originally a band with my brother Syd, but—"

"Oh, Syd Garcia?" The teacher seemed to know him.

"Yeah! He was a guitarist of this band and—"
"He was a pain to teach," she looked at her phone. My smile faded away, "I hope you aren't."

I wanted to say I was way worse.

"Are you sure you're playing for the opening ceremony?"

"Yeah." I already lost interest.

"Who else is in your band?"

"Sachiko, Emmie, Alex," I pointed to each member.

"And Maya."

The teacher shot her laser eyes at Maya, who awkwardly waved and smiled at her.

"Did Mr. Reyes tell you what time to go up?"

"Ahh, yeah, actually," I brought out my tablet to track the original email he sent last night, "8 am?"

The teacher said nothing before turning around to look at the big digital clock above the big white board.

7:50 am. Fudge.

I stood up so quickly that my hip hit the desk, making a loud bang.

"Lu, calm down!" Maya shouted from the front. Alex groggily woke up from her nap and dragged herself to her guitar bag. Sachiko brought her iPad with her as she skipped outside the room with Maya. Emmie, Alex, and I got our guitar bags and rushed out the room. We ran like we hit a star in Mario Kart, rushing up the stairs at max speed.

Behind us, the teacher clapped her hands and shouted, "Okay, girls! Form two lines so we can watch Masks Out play."

"Stupid teacher," I muttered under my breath.

We reached the music room on the fifth floor but it was empty and the gym on the sixth was slowly becoming chaotic, so we all turned to the next flight of stairs. We almost collided with Mr. Reyes.

"Sir, we are so sorry for being late," I apologized almost involuntarily. Everyone stood behind me, fiddling their guitar bags and nodding.

"No, no, it's not about that," he sighed. "I wanted to apologize, too for... um..."

"What is it, sir?" Maya asked. Mr. Reyes did not have to respond as we all heard the deafening sound coming from above us.

"St. Teresa Academy! Make. Some. Noooooise!" My eyes narrowed at Mr. Reyes.

That voice. I know that voice. That's—

"Shit."

I rushed up the stairs, holding the bottom of my guitar bag to stop it from wobbling off my back. We reached the gym's blue door and peeked at the small glass window. On the big stage stood three galaxy-colored girls. Below them are the students and teachers cheering for them.

The moths in my stomach flew up and tickled my throat with their dusty wings as I laid eyes on the vocalist and bassist.

"Are you okay, Lu?" Maya's soft voice perked up as she lightly placed her left hand on my shoulder. The other three girls squished in to get a better view of the stage.

"Dani..."

My voice trailed off, slowly I backed away and watched Sachiko get my spot. I threw down a look of betrayal at Mr. Reyes and he lowered his head as he waited at the bottom of the stairs.

"Shut up! Is this Timestarterz?" Alex curved her hands around her eyes as if she held binoculars, making it easier for her to see through the glass.

"Timestarterz?" Maya repeated.

"They're this new trio that formed over the summer and gained a lot of popularity after their debut," Sachiko dug her phone out her pocket and began to film. "Martha's on drums."

"Debut..." I repeated slowly.

There was a girl who played at the very back of the stage, behind the vocalist. Her long, frizzy hair was pulled up in a tall ponytail, the rest of her hair covered her face, which moved just as much as her wrists that held onto the drumsticks for dear life. She looked forward, smiling, mouthing the lyrics, making funny faces at whoever in our audience locked eyes with her.

"Ooh! Carla's the girl on the synthesizer!" Sachiko's voice raised by a decibel. I watched her as she lifted herself off to stand on tiptoe. I pursed my lips when I saw her sparkly eyes.

The girl she called Carla moved her fingers so professionally across the keyboard, pressing buttons with her free hand to create completely different sound. She would look at her keyboard, then nod at Martha before smiling at the audience.

"Theeeeen..." Sachiko wasn't done, "And there she is." She tried to lift her soles even higher hoping this would make her taller. Slipping expectedly, she gave a small squeal before landing softly on the ground. I caught her just on time.

"Careful, Sach," I warned her softly. She dusted her skirt, nodding.

"Thanks," she stood up and rushed back to her spot, "As I was saying, there she—"

"Is," I finished her sentence apathetically, "Dani Gonzales."

The four looked at me, "You know her?" Sachiko asked for everyone.

I turned around, laser beams from my eyes, hoping I could burn the bald man that is Mr. Reyes. Cornering him, I made sure his pitiful eyes were looking at me.

"What made you think getting a band from another school would be better than letting your own school's band play?" I glared at him, waiting for an answer.

"They're popular," he replied, "They have experience playing, and—"

"And what? They're prettier? Did you just see those three girls on Instagram and decided fuck that other band who spent their whole summer practicing for this day?" My heart beat faster, as if it was trying to fly out of my raging chest. I flailed my arms at Mr. Reyes.

"Lu…" Mr. Reyes could not lift his head.

I licked my snaggletooth.

"Listen, sir," I placed my hands on my hips. "Maxxed Out is gonna break records, hold more concerts than our ages combined and get recognized by the greatest of musicians out there." I scoffed at him, "You're gonna freaking regret this."

"Lucy!" Maya shouted my name the same way a mom would to her child if she caught them being disrespectful. "I get that you're mad but have some respect."

The gym door opened. A rather tall and wide lady in slacks and heels came out and smiled at us. It was Ms. Del Rosario, the school dean.

"Lu and company!" She shouted amidst the screams. She was oblivious to the situation as she invited us. "Come on! They're going to sing their last song!"

To my surprise, my four bandmates rushed out into the wide gymnasium, and the screams of the students once again muffled as Ms. Del Rosario closed the door. I looked back at Mr. Reyes who still had his head down. We had nothing left to say so I opened the blue door and entered the concert zone.

The speakers blasted the latest song, even the janitors were dancing. No one was sitting during the three-minute performance. I stayed near the blue wall with most of the teachers. All of them had their phones on, filming the three galaxy girls. I clenched my fists, hiding them inside the pockets of my jacket. I leaned against the wall, taking in this shit they called lyrics.

Faith, trust, and pixie dust
I've got it all up my sleeve

Dani's bass followed the movement of her hips. Her way of strumming the bass strings differed from Emmie's. She used a guitar pick and picked at the strings rather than pluck them with her two fingers. Her smile sent a whole class jumping up and down, screaming.

Captain Hook's slurs won't work on me.
We'll fly up, up, just grab my hand...

She was having a blast. I could see it on her face while looking at the ecstatic crowd. Until she spotted me.

...to Neverland

Her smile stopped. That second felt like an hour. The gym quieted down. Her big brown eyes were on me. They looked at me in disbelief, in shock.

It looked like she was about to stop strumming until a boy screamed, "Dani, marry me!"

Immediately, she was back to performing. She jumped a bit more than usual. Rushing to have a small dance with Carla and Martha during the instrumental.

That glance left a sting.

"You're not joining your friends?" Mr. Lim, our Filipino teacher, leaned a bit close toward my ear to ask. I unclenched my fist, taking my sweaty palms out of my pockets to air out.

"It's because her band was supposed to play," Ms. Chung, the chemistry teacher, explained. Mr. Lim looked at me, then at her.

"Was it the band Mr. Reyes asked? What was the name of their band?" Mr. Lim asked.

"I don't know," Ms. Chung replied. "Lu, what was the name of your band?" The two looked at me.

"Maxxed Out," I mumbled. They exchanged glances, shocked at remembering the name.

"Isn't that Syd's band?" Mr. Lim whispered.

"I thought that band was gone after he—" Ms. Chung skimmed my face for an answer.

"I reformed the band with better members," I answered, my eyes now looking at my feet.

"There you are, Lu." I looked at our teacher, Imelda Santos according to her ID, and stood up straight.

"Their band was supposed to perform?" Mr. Lim brought Ms. Santos into the conversation. She did not look too happy to be a part of it.

"As claimed by this young lady who is supposed to be with her class."

I sighed as I speedwalked to the front of the stage to find my classmates. Ms. Santos walked behind me. Silently, I stood next to Emmie, which wasn't a good idea because I looked like a garden gnome next to her. Turning my head away from her and from the band, I took in my other classmates who seemed to have a blast. They would have screamed like this with our band, I sighed.

Turning to look at my bandmates, I saw that they watched the performance silently. Kind of felt like it was my fault they acted like this, but another part of me wanted to believe that they were thinking of how it could have been them performing on stage.

"St. Teresa, thaaaank yooou!" Dani shouted before turning to Martha behind her.

Martha played a quick drum solo that clashed yet harmonized with Carla's beat from the synthesizer. Dani joined in on the craziness playing her own bass solo. The three wrapped it up with a loud whack on the drums, and the fading of Carla's instrument. The crowd stood up, jumping and cheering for a job well done. I heard my bandmates mumbling something while clapping.

"...ask the keyboardist..." I heard a bit of Sachiko.

"...silently...Lu might..." I heard a bit of Alex.

"Why is she..." I heard a bit of Emmie.

"I'll go with…" I heard a bit of Maya.

"Okay, girls," Ms. Santos called our attention. "First row, go down, followed by second row."

"Ms. Imelda!" Mr. Reyes jogged up to her, his hands waving. "Can you let Lu's group stay back?"

Ms. Santos looked at each of us. Maya gave a nervous smile, waving awkwardly. Alex looked around the gymnasium. Sachiko looked down at her feet. Emmie turned to look at me. I stared straight at Mr. Reyes, who was looking around the gymnasium too.

"Okay then, Raffy," she told Mr. Reyes before addressing us. "Be down right away." She turned her back and followed the second row of students down the stairs. The gymnasium was slowly growing quiet as students went back to their classes.

"Hi, girls!" Mr. Reyes nervously laughed. Maya joined in but her face froze after seeing our stoic faces. "Lu, come with me," he continued.

I slowly walked forward, turning around to see if my bandmates were behind me. In a line, we followed Mr. Reyes backstage where amplifiers scattered and wires intertwined and crawled under the platform, resembling veins. Three galaxy girls walked a few steps toward us, their heels made soft clanking sounds. They stopped in front of Mr. Reyes who moved away from us to stand beside them, revealing Dani's face to me. Both of us took sharp breaths at the same time.

"Here is our school's band I wanted to introduce to you," Mr. Reyes acted as if he could not read the atmosphere. "Lu, would you want to introduce yourselves?"

Dani spoke first, "Maxxed Out still exists?" She tilted her head innocently. "I thought the band was gone five years ago."

"It's been thriving," I bluffed. "I found people who actually want to play." Dani gulped, looking taken aback. The other members of both bands looked around the gymnasium, avoiding my serious expression and Dani's.

"W-w-well," Mr. Reyes stepped in, "It seems you know each other. Were you in Maxxed Out, too?" Emmie, Alex, and Sachiko all looked at her, anticipating her answer.

"No," Dani lied with a smile. A knife pierced my heart. "I just heard about them when I was younger." My bandmates were wary of my expression. I looked like I could kill someone. I bit the inside of my cheeks hard.

"Nice!" Mr. Reyes was walking on thin ice trying to lighten the atmosphere. "Well, the reason I asked you girls to meet was because… ahh…Dani, would you like to tell Lu and her bandmates what you told me?"

Dani fixed her sweet smile and said, "My mom told me that my band should join the Battle of the Bands! I was hoping you and your band would join. I would be very excited to play against you."

I scoffed. "Sure," I agreed, leaning a bit forward and narrowing my eyes, "We'd beat your asses in a second." My bandmates sighed at my threat.

"Hey, relax there, chibi," Alex pulled my shoulder— and my whole body— back.

"Please tell me you're joking," Emmie rubbed the bridge of her nose.

"Lu, please," Maya softly pleated.

I kept my eyes on Dani's. Curse those brown eyes. "Curse them," I whispered under my breath.

"What was that?" Mr. Reyes showed his white pearls. His sweat was visible front and back of his bald head. Timestarterz definitely had a blast seeing a shiny bald head, and sweat trickling and dripping onto the floor. He vigorously wiped his head with his handkerchief, waiting for me to repeat my sentence.

"Can you give us the info for this battle of the bands?" I asked him calmly.

"Oh, of course," He looked relieved at my question. He fumbled through his pockets and produced a black flyer. I took it from him, it read:

BATTLE OF THE BANDS
Open to all high school bands
Sancta Caecilia's School of Fine Arts

My band looked at me, waiting for a sign of approval. Dani's band and Mr. Reyes waited as well.

"Well?" Mr. Reyes stretched his neck, begging for an answer. My eyes met Dani's dull brown eyes. I took my time stuffing the flyer into the pocket of my jacket, giving her one more glare before walking back to my classroom. Emmie, Alex, and Maya nervously jogged to catch up with me. Sachiko stayed behind for a bit. I could hear her starting a conversation with the other band. Blocking the noise, I stared at my black shoes, lifting and landing on the off-white stairs. My mind was filled with rage and screams echoed in my head. All I could think of was Dani.

"Sorry, I took late!" Sachiko caught up with the four of us. She went down the steps a bit quicker to walk on my side.

She saw my smirk, so she stayed quiet. Emmie, Maya, and Alex sparked a conversation between themselves about homework. I continued to stare at my black shoes. Wham! I bumped into a boy who was going the opposite direction.

"Sorry!" He yelled as he apologized.

"No, no, don't swe—" I broke off once I saw the boy's face. My face burned. My inside burned. Emmie, Sachiko, Alex, and Maya stopped in their tracks, all eyes widening at the familiar face.

"Hey, Lu," Emmie tapped my shoulder. "Don't we know this boy?"

"The pizza boy," Sachiko whispered under her breath.

"Thank you for the pizza the other day," Maya smiled.

"What was his name again? Aries? Aether?" Alex furrowed her eyebrows and rubbed her chin. Emmie nudged her.

"Luh… where did you get those names?" Emmie snickered. Alex laughed back. Maya shushed them both.

"His name is Aerol," I said.

"Lu," Aerol oddly looked relieved to see me. "Didn't think you'd be here at St. Teresa's."

I scratched my back as I stared at the floor behind him. "Didn't think you'd be here either," I mumbled. I could hear the four at the back whisper something among themselves.

"I've been meaning to ask you," Aerol clasped his hands together. He licked his lips.

"Shut up! A confession?!" Maya's small voice grew a bit louder. She held Alex's arm tightly and shook it. "Shet—wait, wait, waaait!"

Her fangirling made me dread whatever Aerol was going to ask me. I pursed my lips, bracing myself for the worst thing he could ask. We were friends since we were five, plus he was part of the original four in Maxxed Out with Syd. He was a favorite of my mom (and my mom is absolutely hesitant of any boy I mention) and was always the mediator whenever Dani and I would get into a fight. It would be totally understandable if he did end up developing feelings for me. But ever since that last fight with Dani, I doubt it.

"Oh my god can you ask her already?" Emmie was getting impatient. "We have a class to attend!"

"And a whole year of teasing her," Alex added. Once again, Maya who was still wrapped tight around Alex's arm, shushed her.

"Lu," Aerol started. Shit, here it comes.

"Have you already entered the math camp my mom told your mom about?" He looked like a five-year old, all excited and looking forward to hearing a 'yes' come out of my mouth.

"Are you serio—" Maya had never sounded more disappointed.

"Booo!" Alex cupped her mouth.

I turned around and glared at them. They stopped immediately. Relieved, I turned back to Aerol.

"Excuse my bandmates," I apologized. "Ah...you know...my mom didn't see the...the...email. Yes, the email!" Aerol gave me a weird look.

"But my mom sent it two weeks ago," Aerol slightly tilted his head the same way Dani did, "Should I have my mom resend it to her?"

"No! No, no, no, no, no, —" I chanted, shaking my head furiously. "My mom...ah...ch-checked it already!"

"You just said she didn't—"

"And then I remembered she did!" I grabbed Alex's wrist and walked past him. "Dani's upstairs."

Back in the classroom, I dragged my guitar bag next to my desk and slid into my chair. Lowering my head, I rummaged for that reply slip I shoved in the bag this morning. I transferred the slip from my left to my right so I could slide my left hand into the front pocket of my guitar bag to grab Syd's birthday card. I did not bother reading it. I let the sides of my pointer and middle finger rub the material. The birthday card used cardstock and was pretty durable. The reply slip on the other hand was already crumpled and rolled up, all creases and folds. The paper rolled around my finger the more I rubbed it. It makes sense. I trusted my brother's words more than anyone in this world.

My thoughts went back to Aerol and Dani. What good would seeing them do me? I sighed, shoved the two papers in each pocket, and rested my head on my arms then looked at my bandmates.

Emmie was diagonal to me. She was probably playing co-op with Sachiko who sat next to me. The two looked way too focused on their identical looking screens to notice a group of volleyball girls with slim bodies and messy buns walk up to Emmie.

"Looks like Maxxed Out really stayed out," Pat, the volleyball captain remarked.

I sighed at her stupid joke. Emmie remained unbothered, only her fingers and her mouth moving to whisper shit when her fingers weren't quick enough to touch all the notes coming at her.

"Yeah, and what about it," Emmie had her eyes glued to her screen like Sachiko, another quick shit escaped her mouth.

"I don't know," Pat removed her light blue scrunchie and ruffled her long, wavy hair. "Maybe being a bassist isn't doing it for you."

Emmie paused her game. Sachiko did the same. Emmie looked straight at Pat's eyes.

"You think this is how you're going to convince me to join your team?" Emmie rested her head on her right hand, waiting for Pat to continue speaking even if her expression was of pure indignation.

"Come on, Ems," Pat crouched down and held the edge of Emmie's table with her finger tips, trying to look cute. "You're such a great setter! Plus, I doubt this high school phase of a band is going to get you anywhere."

"Pat, watch what you're saying," her friend Ari nudged her. "Lu's watching."

This time, a shit escaped my lips. I shifted my gaze to appear like I was sleeping. Pat scoffed.

"You relay this message to your band, 'kay?" Pat stood up, tapping Emmie's desk with her nail. Emmie nodded, turning around to ask Sachiko if they could restart the song they were playing.

No one had to grab a hoodie because of the aircon. They've got my anger to keep them warm.

As far as I know, Emmie was interested in volleyball and Maya in Math. I know she used to play back in fourth grade, but she stopped around the time I recruited her. Since then, she was silent about playing for our school even if, according to rumors, she was one of the best players.

Screw them, my brain grumbled, screw them all. Screw them for underestimating us. We'll show them. We'll show them all! I tightened my grip on the sleeves of my jacket. We'll beat Timestarterz's asses and we'll win first in that freaking concert.

"How are we going to beat them?" I did not notice Maya was crouching right next to me.

"What does Lu's Laboratory have in store for us?" Alex sat cross legged on the floor next to her.

Staring at both of them, I slowly lifted my head up and sat up straight. I noticed Sachiko turned off her iPad to listen to what I had to say, and Emmie turned around to join the conversation.

"We're going straight to the clubhouse after school," I ordered. "No excuses."

I looked at their shocked faces. Their mouths formulating a complaint to address.

"Lu, are you sure about this?" Maya asked in disbelief.

"We have to kick their asses," I grumbled, glaring at each one of them to make sure my point was clear. I want Maxxed Out to be on the stage as the main attraction, not as some clickbait for some pop singers who think they make music.

Maya pursed her lips and nodded. No one said another word.

♪♪

It was around 3:10 pm when class ended. While everyone else was too busy chatting and bidding everyone farewell, we were stuffing our materials into our bags, grabbing our instruments, and making our way to the clubhouse. It was as if we were late for an opening ceremony as we ran along the school corridors and jumped into my car at the pickup area.

"We must be the first ones to leave," Maya noticed as we slowly moved away from the empty school entrance.

"Yo, Sach," Alex emerged from the back of the car, resting her arms on the second row of seats where Sachiko, Emmie, and I sat. "Let me use the hotspot."

"Guess the password then," Sachiko let out a little laugh. Alex groaned.

"Ugh, it's your favorite character from Star Beats," Alex closed her eyes tight, trying to remember the name of the character.

"Psssh, isn't that easy?" I scoffed. "It's definitely, ah…" Shit, this is hard.

"It's definitely who, Miss Lu?" Alex mocked me, leaning to hear my answer.

"The guitarist."

"Which one?"

"Shit, ah…um…" Fuck, think of a Japanese name! A Japanese name! "Ran?"

There was silence. I knew Sachiko raised her brows at my response. Alex busted out the loudest snort that made the three girls explode in laughter.

"Why," I nervously asked. "What's up?"

"Lu, no one in Star Beats is named Ran," Alex wiped her tears. "I don't even play it, but I've seen Sachiko play it enough to know that no one in the franchise is named Ran."

"She recites the fanchant while playing sometimes," Emmie added, making Sachiko hide her face in embarrassment.

"Wait, she does?" I asked.

"Oh gosh, this made my afternoon," Maya exhaled. "It's surprising you've never heard Sachiko recite the game's fanchant. She does it at least once every day."

"Oh really?" I laughed it off. I noticed the clubhouse a few blocks away. "Guys, get ready."

Like the Beatles running away from the paparazzi, we jumped out of the car, carrying our bags as we rushed toward the glass door that led to Room 112, our rented practice room.

No words were exchanged. We immediately threw away our school bags on the floor and rushed to the center of the room. Emmie, Alex, and I waddled to our positions while unzipping our instruments from their guitar bags. Sachiko and Maya requested to borrow a spare set of drums and keyboard from RJ, who was nice enough to let them use both for as long as they needed to. The two jogged to their stations, warming up while waiting for us three to finish tuning our guitars and bass.

I placed a quick chord progression of C–F–G–Bm before confirming that my guitar was tuned correctly.

"Is everyone ready?" I stared at the mirror to catch everyone nodding at their respective instruments.

"Reptilia on three."

"One! Two! Three! Go!" Maya banged her drumsticks together. Once I heard the first bang of her drumsticks against the drum, I started to omit a steady beat from my guitar. We went at it for a while as Alex's guitar faded in and soon, she began to play the melody. Emmie joined in with her bass, assisting Maya in carrying a steady beat as I changed to another strumming pattern. Sachiko gave the song a character by playing long notes that were similar in chord. The whole intro flowed well. When it was time for me to sing, I stepped a bit forward to the mic and began to recite the lyrics.

He seemed impressed by the way you came in.

I winced mid-sentence. I caught onto something: someone was not in sync. I closed my eyes for the entire line, making sure my ears were able to make each instrument stand out to detect who was not catching up.

Tell us a story, I know you're not—

It's Maya.

"Damn it, Maya!" I shouted.

The drumsticks fell. Alex let her guitar hang loose. Emmie immediately turned around, holding the neck of her bass. Sachiko rested her fingers on the keys she last touched. There was silence.

"Lu, I'm sorry," Maya spoke too quickly. I knew she was trying to hold back her tears. I let out a silent laugh. The members looked at me, worried at what I was going to do or say next.

"This is freaking stupid," I laughed. I turned around, taking a sharp breath. "This is freaking stupid! We worked our asses off for what could have been our first step to greatness, so what? A bunch of artificial barbies could take our spotlight? Great. Just freaking great. Just. Freaking. Great! Why are you not mad? A bunch of rip offs just shoved your asses off your own goddamn stage! I don't get it! We! Were! So! Fucking! Close! We were so close t—"

Alex's hard slap stung my cheek. I could not help but be silent. Maya finally broke down in soft hiccups. Emmie rushed to hug her while Sachiko placed all her attention on the crying drummer than the two aggravated guitarists.

"You and Syd were so close," Alex corrected me.

Her eyes were dead set on mine with no intention of looking elsewhere. Her dark brown pupils stabbed me like knives while her slow, low voice trembled with anger.

"We weren't even near the words almost, dumbass."

She motioned to slap me once more. I flinched. My legs felt like noodles. I dropped down to the floor, trying to catch my breath. No words were spoken. Alex brought down her hand, lightly placing her guitar back into its bag and zipping it up. Emmie rushed to put her bass back in its bag, too. With one arm holding the bag's strap and the other rubbing Maya's back, Emmie followed Alex out of the room. Sachiko turned the keyboard off and her phone on, walking to grab her bag and whispering kutabare before walking out. Alex glanced at me, in a puddle on the floor, before slamming the door.

Silence.

I stared at the lonely drum set. It hasn't even been an hour since we arrived, let alone 20 minutes. Everything happened so quickly. My heart was beating loudly. I stared at the white ceiling and the microphone stand that was still plugged in. I twisted my head to the mirror.

I could hear my brother telling me, "You're alone again, Lu. Did something happen to you and your friends? You had another fight? It's okay, Lu."

I felt my breathing grow unstable, like Maya's a few minutes ago. I began to sob softly. I could not stop crying. I shielded my eyes from the light, my hands forming into fists of frustration.

Syd would say, "It's okay to cry it out. That means you still cherish them."

I turned to my side and curled up into a ball, the same way I would when Syd would let me cry on his bed. My sobs were louder than my thoughts.

"Kuya," I whispered in between the sobbing, "I'm a failure."

"Lu?" The voice was familiar.

Slowly, I opened my eyes and noticed I wasn't in my room. I did not bother sitting up. Instead, I stared blankly at the brown ceiling, noticing the sound of the wind and kids chatting from outside. I tried recalling everything that led me up to this specific moment.

Everything was a blur.

The bed creaked so I directed my focus at the boy sitting at the edge of my bed.

"Aerol!?" I croaked.

"Thank goodness, you're awake!" He seemed relieved.

"What the heck happened to me?"

"The counselor told me to stay with you until you wake up," he did not answer my question. "I'll wait outside the cabin. I brought you fresh clothes, by the way. Hurry up though. It's time for our group meeting!"

With that, he stood up and left. The loud chatter of kids muffled once again as he closed the door. I took a few lazy seconds to stare blankly at the ceiling one last time, just to remember what happened.

Well, I fought with my bandmates, might've caused our disbandment, and now I'm here waking up to Aerol talking about something I don't know. I furrowed my eyebrows, remembering what he just said.

Counselor. Cabin. Group meeting. Oh! In a flash, I sat up, now totally awake.

I noticed a dark blue shirt, a pair of shorts, and a fresh pair of undergarments folded neatly near the foot of the bed. Looking down, I noticed I was not in my school uniform either. I was in a white shirt I never knew I owned. Odd, I thought to myself.

Time must not be wasted any further. I leaned over to reach the folded shirt and unfolded it to see what the design was. A butterfly with handprints as wings in white on the left breast. On the back, each letter of Bayanihan in red, green, and white squares located at the center of the shirt. My eyes widened upon realization of my whereabouts.

"Oh shit," I mumbled. I heard an aggressive knock on my door.

"Uy, bilisan mo!" Aerol screamed from outside. "Ba't ang bagal?"

"Have some patience, will you?" I grumbled as I changed my clothes. I looked at the empty bed in front of me. It was a mess. Clothes were scattered on the floor and on the crumpled sheets of the bed. Whoever she was, my roommate was messy as hell.

I rolled off the bed, feeling the air on my legs and the cold floor on my feet. I fixed my bed, shoving my dirty clothes under the covers as I was running out of time, grabbed my socks and sneakers and walked out the door.

"You took so long," Aerol commented. I sat down to properly put on my shoes.

"Dude, I needed time to process," I slapped his leg. "Bastos."

Aerol laughed, "Glad you could make it."

"Did I have a choice in the first place?"

"Mmm...well, yeah, I guess," Aerol smirked. "Your mom emailed the camp quicker than you could decide."

I sighed angrily. Curse you, mom.

Aerol patted my back, "It'll be great, Lu! Tita Mads always wanted you to get out of the house and get some fresh air."

More like she's always wanted me out, period.

♪♪

"Goood morning, camperrrs!" A blonde lady in her early 20s shouted through a megaphone. "Lovely seeing everyone here at Bayanihan!" The energetic voice gave me headaches. Why am I here?

"This doesn't look like a math camp," I told Aerol.

"Because it isn't?"

"Are you serious?" I slouched. "All the more that this whole thing is freaking stupid." He patted my back.

"Lighten up, Lu," he said as he looked at the lady with the megaphone. "It'll be fine."

"Oh, you know what would be great?" I gritted my teeth, "staying at home playing my guita—"

"You there! Hi!" The lady jogged toward me.

"Ah...hi?" I greeted back.

"You two know each other?" She pointed to Aerol then to me.

"Yes, we do," Aerol squinted at her name tag.

"Miss... Elizabeth?"

"Oh, just call me Ellie," she smiled. "Or Els if you're feeling cool." She pointed finger guns at the two of us. I kept looking at her, poker faced.

"I was hoping that you would be nice enough to introduce yourself to some campers. You know, make new friends while you're here?" She showed us her bunny teeth while waiting for an answer. I exchanged glances with Aerol, giving him a look of hope that he would decline the offer. He looked at me, then smiled at Ellie.

"My friend here would be ecstatic to make some new friends," he said, pushing me forward. I was about to curse him but Ellie quickly took hold of my wrist, thanking me for being so considerate while dragging me to two Japanese girls about my age who were sitting on a nearby bench.

The girl on the right had blonde, wavy hair and bangs that covered her forehead. She tucked her camp shirt inside a pair of high waisted denim jeans and topped her outfit with a pair of sneakers that showed off her ankles. Her sparkly nails held onto her phone that was playing music. She did not bother to look up when Ellie and I arrived.

The other girl gave us a glance before going back to the blonde girl's phone. Her mid-length, brown hair was ties into a quick ponytail, little strands hanging out on the sides of her face. She wore her camp shirt loose over a pair of leggings and running sneakers. She wore arm sleeves to cover her pale skin from the sun. It was interesting to see how contrasting the two girls were dressed.

"Hi!" Ellie greeted them to grab their attention. They seemed to be engrossed in a video on the phone, but calmly turned off the screen to listen to what she had to say. "This lovely bud right here wishes to get to know you!"

She held both my shoulders and smiled at me as she whispered, "I'll leave you three to chat."

Once Ellie left, the girls resumed watching the video as I stood in front of them, cursing every adult I've met. Including Aerol.

I could be practicing by myself for that competition. I could go solo and show Dani what real music is. Hah! I'll watch her pathetic ass walk out the door, rethinking her decisions. Kuya will be so proud. The idea made me smile. Revenge is best served cold, right? Of course, I would only be doing that if mom had not put me in this dumb camp.

I scanned the open space — kids and counselors were scattered across the ground. There was a basketball court and the mess hall was to the west. Zero idea what was beyond the mess hall, but I could recognize a big tree on a hill.

Sighing, I spotted Aerol on the gravel steps near the court. He was chatting with a brown-skinned boy holding a guitar, both seemed to be enjoying the conversation. Aerol turned around and locked eyes with mine. He gave me a suck-it-up kind of smirk and pointed to the two Japanese girls with his lips. He then widened his eyes as if telling me to "Go talk to them. Now.' I pouted. Aerol smiled, shook his head, and placed all his attention on the boy he was chatting with.

Looking back at the girls, the one with the ponytail patted the spot next to her. She nudged the blonde girl holding the phone, mumbling something in Japanese. With a shy smile, I thanked her and quickly sat down next to her.

For once, my legs were stuck together. Not even in school did I sit like a lady. At least one leg had to be bent up for my chin to rest on. Wow. Summer camp could change you. My eyes soon turned to the screen that the two girls were viewing. The screen showed five older girls, probably the same age as Ellie, seated on a long table, watching two younger girls who were most likely around my age on the main stage playing a rhythm game. I did not want to lean forward to see better, I was already worried I was too awkward. I stared at my hands that had not moved from my knees. I bit my cheek.

I told myself that if I had an easy time going up to my bandmates, it'll be a breeze to start a conversation with these girls. Alright! I looked forward, took a deep breath. And—

"Wh— whatcha wa— watching?" I paused, closed my eyes, and regretted my stuttering.

The blonde girl gave me a cold stare, but luckily the girl who offered me the spot gave me a somewhat reassuring smile. She turned her head at the blonde girl, whispering something to her. With a roll of her eyes, the blonde girl turned her phone toward me.

"I'm Lu, by the way. You are?"

"I'm Yukari," the girl with the ponytail smiled politely before gesturing her hand to the blonde girl. "She is…" Yukari gave the blonde girl a nudge using her elbow.

The blonde girl sighed, "Sayaka."

"Yukari," I pointed at Yukari. She nodded. "Sayaka," I pointed to Sayaka. Yukari nodded for her. Then we all went back to watching the livestream video.

Three young girls at the center of the stage, yelling sugoi or haya sugiru. Older girls clapping for them. I noticed standees at the back: anime characters equipped with instruments like guitars, keyboards, or drumsticks. I also noticed a familiar star — with rings and a few music notes floating around it — on the jacket of one of the older girls.

"Star Beats?"

"You know them?" Yukari looked surprised. Sayaka did not pay any mind.

"Pshh, yeah," I bluffed. Yukari turned to Sayaka, nudging her and whispering something in Japanese.

"Who's your favorite member?" Sayaka asked, finally looking at me. Her cold stare held me at gunpoint, waiting for a good answer. Shit.

"Ahh, Ran...?"

"Ran!?" Sayaka raised an eyebrow. Yukari nervously glanced at me, and gave out a nervous laugh and a pitiful smile.

"Lu, no one in Star Beats is named Ran," she told me. Shit.

"Oh! I-I-ah...I meant—"

"Nice try, loser," Sayaka went back to viewing the livestream. Yukari looked tense, nudging her and nervously laughing.

"Come on, Sayaka," Yukari seemed to say in Japanese.

Yah, cut me some slack. Please.

Sayaka rolled her eyes, "Kutabare." For some reason, the way Sayaka said it was way scarier than how Sachiko said it.

Yukari turned to me, "Sorry. She's just annoyed she hasn't met anyone who likes this game as much as she does."

"Oh, it's totally understandable," I said. "I would feel the same way." Sayaka gave both of us a long glare before going back to her screen.

The video was showing older girls walking up to the area where the winner stood. They were congratulating her while the girls exchanged bows and compliments. One of the older girls gestured to the winner to introduce herself to the viewers.

"Hello! I'm 14 years old and I am from Osaka. Fujiwara Sachiko!" The winner introduced herself. I stood up with disbelief.

"Sachiko?!" Yukari was worried. Sayaka was disgusted.

"Yeah…" Sayaka was already sick of me. "Never heard of her?"

"She's my bandmate!"

Sayaka almost dropped her phone. Yukari's jaws dropped. "Are you serious?!" Sayaka stood up to retrieve her phone.

"Sayaka is obsessed with her," Yukari stood up too. "She's all she ever talks about." Sayaka crossed her arms and rolled her eyes.

"I'm just a big fan," Sayaka sassily corrected her. "There's a difference."

"Yeah," Yukari nodded with a sarcastic smile.

"Wait," I was still confused. "When did she— how did she— I could've sworn she was—"

"You didn't know?" Sayaka asked. She gave me the same glare when I could not name a character from Star Beats.

"She must've told you," Yukari said. "You're her friend, right?" She side-eyed Sayaka at the word friend.

I looked down at the ground. What was I supposed to say? "Yeah, she definitely told us, but I was too busy playing my guitar to care about her whereabouts."

Sayaka exited the livestream to search up a channel on YouTube. The banner at the top of the page was soft teal with chibi drawings of Star Beats characters. Underneath the Japanese characters read "Starry Sachiko." I looked at the profile photo, that of an anime character (most probably her favorite one from the game), and the number of subscribers she had underneath her channel name. 198k subscribers. "Holy shit," I mumbled.

"Sachiko never told you about her YouTube channel?" Yukari emphasized how horrible of a friend I was.

"Well…"

"How is Sachiko as a bandmate?" Sayaka sounded interested. "She must be very cooperative and willing to dance a style that's not really her favorite."

Yukari rolled her eyes. Sayaka smirked as if she had won this battle of passive aggression.

I sighed, "When Sach gets into something, she talks nonstop about it." I sat down, already drained thinking about it. "She's been chatting about some keyboardist from this dumb artificial band who played at our school. Their music is so coated with fake flavorings it could make you sick."

"Hah! Kinda like Sayaka," Yukari laughed, receiving a kick from Sayaka. "Oh, but Lu, I have a question."

"Go."

"Are you talking about Timestarterz?" Yukari asked.

"Heard about them?" I asked.

"Yeah," Yukari answered. "We actually just talked to—"

I felt someone tap my shoulder. It was Aerol.

"Yo, Lu," he pointed to the boy he was talking to. "Got someone you should meet." I said my quick goodbyes to Sayaka and Yukari and followed Aerol. The two girls did not seem bothered anyway and went back to viewing the livestream.

Aerol led me to the steps near the court. The boy was waiting for us and his face broke into a big grin. Up close, he was tall. Like, Aerol tall. And that's tall.

"This is Lu," Aerol patted my shoulder. The boy could not stop smiling as he reached out his hand. "I told him about your band. He's really ecstatic to meet you," Aerol continued the introduction.

"Benefits of having Aerol as a roommate," his voice was quite husky, and there was something about his smile that felt very uplifting. "You must be the guitarist."

I gave Aerol a confused look before shaking his hand, "Ah...yes."

"I'm Aiden! You?"

"Lu."

"Like Luna from Breaking Daylights?"

I raised an eyebrow, glancing at Aerol again, wondering if he told Aiden something else. "Uh...no?"

I caught Aerol shaking his head at Aiden, making him stop smiling as his eyes widened like he saw something scary. He went back to his positive expression once he turned back to me.

"Sorry, big fan of the band," his hand was still holding mine. "You should give them a listen."

I focused on his warm hand, giving my lonely one a home, "Mmm. Yeah."

Aiden noticed it, and immediately let go, "Sorry!" He laughed nervously. "So, um...you...signing up for any activities?"

Activity?

"Kid just mentally got here," Aerol crossed his arms. "Uy, check your pockets."

I placed my hand slowly into the short's pocket and pulled out a green paper. Unfolding it, I read the letters written in bold.

Bayanihan Club / Activity Sign-up Sheet

One thing that never changed about Aerol. He was always prepared.

"Well..." I shoved the paper back into my pocket. "How about you?"

Aiden scratched his arm, "I actually wanted to join the Mu—"

A kid yanked Aiden's arm before he could finish his statement. The kid's pale limb contrasted against Aiden's dusky complexion.

"You! You're good at basketball," he said confidently.

I felt a sting of anger, seeing Aiden's scared expression as his eyes darted from the boy to me and then to Aerol. Poor Aiden could not even say shit. He was immediately dragged down to the basketball court by that insolent kid. Aiden turned to give us a nervous smile as he waved goodbye.

"Looks like he found something," Aerol could not keep his eyes off Aiden. I tried to change the topic.

"Have you thought of joining anything?" I brought out the crumpled sign-up sheet.

"Oh, yeah," Aerol got the paper from my hands, straightened it, and looked for a certain activity. Finding it, he pointed to it aggressively, making sure my eyes read it, "Matema-kicks: the camp's math club for math wizards." I clenched my fists at the word math. Aerol noticed it and ruffled my hair. "Join me na, loser."

"I'm not a loser," I grumbled. "You just really sound like my mom right now."

"Isn't that why you're here?" Aerol patted my shoulder. I sighed.

"This is freaking ridi—"

"Hey, hey! Ease up on the vocabulary," Ellie caught me. I felt my cheeks turn red. She smiled.

"I wasn't here for that — oh, yeah! Come on kids! The talent show is about to start!" She shouted the same thing to the basketball kids down the steps. Ellie gave us one more smile before walking toward the center of the campsite.

"I'm tired of this shit," I mumbled. I tried to walk away from Aerol so I could make a run to the cabin, but he yanked my arm.

"Where do you think you're going?"

I groaned, "This is stupid!"

"Only stupid people think stuff like 'this is stupid,'" he smirked. I rolled my eyes. "You know I'm just pulling your leg, right?"

"You're actually pulling my ar—"

"Oh, my gosh. Why are you such a killjoy?" Aerol laughed. I took a whole tour of my brain at his remark. "Lighten up, math genius. Come on, let's watch na."

"Fine," I groaned. I let him drag me toward the area where all the other kids gathered. Ellie stood on an elevated surface.

"Hello once again campers!" Her energetic voice made me want to puke. "Did everyone enjoy the small chit-chat sesh? Now we're going to have a small talent show!"

She gestured to us to clap at her announcement. After five seconds of clapping, she made sure the campers were still listening before talking again.

"Okay now, we're open for contestants!" She gave a weird look. "Not that this is a competition. This is just a little get-to-know-you type of activity! Don't be shy kids, step on up!"

"I can't bear to watch this," I told Aerol.

"Then how about you go?" Aerol suggested. "Probably the closest thing you'll get to playing your guitar."

"Are you serious?" I widened my eyes at him. I really hoped he was joking. His facial expression remained stoic, as he looked forward, listening to Ellie.

"I will take serious measures in three…" he counted.

"Aerol, what are you going to do—"

"Two…"

"Aerol," I inched away from him, scared. "Aerol don't—"

"One," he poked my sides. I gave a loud yelp and stood up.

"You there!" Ellie pointed at me. "Lovely entrance."

I clenched my fists, shooting lasers at Aerol. I felt as angry as when Maya screwed up the beat. Once I remembered her crying face, my fists relaxed. I pursed my lips, closing my eyes tight. Everyone was already staring at me. I was the first volunteer too.

God take me away from here.

Eyes on the muddy ground, I marched my way to the elevated platform. Ellie looked really relieved that I had gone up.

"You there," she turned to me. "What's your name again?"

"Lu," my voice was barely a whisper.

"Your pronouns?" I looked at her.

"Mmm...she/her...nothing much," I mumbled.

"And what do you have prepared for us, Lu?"

"Guitar..."

Ellie bent down and whispered, "Sweetie, are you okay? You don't have to do this if you don't want to."

I wish I took that offer, but I was a stubborn piece of shit. I looked at her and shook my head. I heard steps approaching me, turning around, I noticed the white kid who yanked Aiden away offered me a guitar. He smiled, pushing the instrument toward me.

He left before I could thank him correctly. I watched him sit in between two other boys who must've been his teammates as they were nudging and laughing at him. Sighing and shaking my head, I hung the strap over my head, holding the neck in place. I stared at my sneakers, thinking of a song to sing. I took a deep breath, Arctic Monkeys it is.

I positioned my left fingers to a D minor, and prepared my right fingers to strum. Looking up at the group of kids one last time, I strummed the guitar strongly, and heard a disgusting note come out. Confused, I checked the positioning of my fingers. I felt my blood boil upon hearing a group of boys snickering in the crowd. I turned to see that the white kid was the one who was laughing the loudest. He did not seem to stop once he locked eyes with my glare. I made a loud sigh, proceeding to sit down on the elevated platform to tune the guitar. The kids began to talk to pass time. Ellie tried to get everyone to pay attention, but she ended up putting all her attention on me grumpily tuning the guitar. I strummed the guitar continuously to alert everyone the guitar had been properly tuned.

"Let's now give a warm applause to…Luuuuu!" Ellie gestured to everyone to start clapping. I took a deep breath, positioning my fingers to make the D minor chord. In a loud voice, I began to sing.

"I'm going back—" I stopped.

Out of all the times to crack…why now? My legs felt like noodles. I cursed at my tears for blurring my vision. My breathing was slowly getting unstable. There was nowhere to run.

"LUUUUUU…SEEEEEER!" The white kid did not need a megaphone to amplify his voice. Soon his friends joined in.

"LU-SER! LU-SER!"

Hear Me Out

I could not let my tears escape my eyes. Everyone was watching me. For the first time, I hated being in front. I want to go. I have to go. I need to go. I could not find Aerol in the crowd. From the corner of my eye, I saw Ellie walking up to me.

"Lu?" She lightly placed her hand on my shoulder. "Are you o—"

I shoved the guitar to her before running my way back to the cabin, not caring if I stepped on someone's hand or foot. I opened the cabin door and slammed it so hard it echoed. Wiping my tears, I dragged myself onto my bed, plopping face first. It was stupid of me to cry this hard, but it was even more stupid of me to finally understand what my mom had been telling me. Maybe I should stop playing the guitar, even for a bit. Slowly, the tears dried up on my face and my body became heavier. My breathing steadied, and I was off to sleep.

I woke up, worried that I slept too long again. The sun was still shining though. Sighing, I sat up and examined the room.

My luggage was still lying next to my bed. There was a small night table with a lamp. My eyes wandered off to the messy bed across me, clothes still scattered around. The only thing different was that there was a figure near the bed. I could not make out who it was.

"Why aren't you joining the activities?" I asked.

"I'm joining this one," a familiar voice replied. My eyes widened. I felt goosebumps all over my body.

"Dani?" I sounded more annoyed than astounded.

"Delight seeing you here," she sounded like a robot. She brushed her fingers across her slightly messy brown hair, fluffing it up. "Get used to the mess," she gave me a half-smile. "It's something I can't fix."

I gave the loudest groan and plopped back onto my pillow. This nightmare isn't over. I sat back up again, spotting her "fries before guys" tote bag and her one-piece bathing suit tucked into her high waisted shorts.

"Where are y—"

"Swimming with some of my friends from the ice-breakers," the way she said 'friends' sounded like it was meant to make me feel bad. "Why don't you swim with yours?"

I bit my lips, "You forgot how I—"

"Oh. Is it because you haven't made any friends?" Dani looked at me with a smile. "Sucks for you."

"Why are you so aggressive?" I had to ask.

"Oh, why are you getting so aggro?" She had the audacity to reply. "Anyways feel free to join us." She failed to sound inviting as she stood and left the cabin.

I face-palmed myself so hard I could've sworn my hand left a print over my face. Sighing loudly again, I got out of bed. My toes curled, feeling the cold floor so suddenly. Luckily, my mom packed a pair of Birkenstocks so I slipped these on and walked out of the cabin.

The place looked rather empty aside from the loud chatters coming from afar. I depended on my ears to lead me to wherever the other kids were, past the trees, I figured. The trees reminded me of the seniors back at school though — tall, looming over me, horrific.

The sound grew louder, and before I knew it, I found myself in front of campers having the time of their lives, running after each other, screaming, laughing. Coming here was like entering Hell's restaurant. I guess being roommates with Dani was just an appetizer. And now this was the main course. The freaking meal itself. This is the peak of my nightmare. A swimming pool.

"Lu!" Ellie, Hell's waitress, came up to me. "Hope you're feeling better. Did you bring a swimsuit?"

I placed my hand on my chest to stabilize my breathing, "No…"

"Oh," Ellie pouted and drew a sad face, but immediately gave a comforting smile. "Would you like to just sit next to me then? I'm not swimming."

Something about that smile made me feel a bit better. I let her hold my hand and walk me to the spot filled with seats, board games, drinks, and towels. Justin Timberlake's music blasted on as campers splashed about. Ellie pointed to a white foldable chair, similar to the ones at the village clubhouse. I sat on it and grabbed a cold bottle of C2 from the ice box next to the chair.

"You good like this?" She asked, glancing at the campers in the pool, then at me.

"Yeah," I stared at my Birks. Droplets of water landed inches away from me. I tensed up. Ellie noticed my reaction and immediately looked at the kids who started it.

"Hey!" Her booming voice surprised me. "Watch where you're splashing, 'kay?"

The kids looked at her miserably, before swimming away from us. Ellie then crouched next to me, hand on my shoulder once again.

"Is there anything you want to tell me?" She gently asked. I tensed up even more, embarrassed of my phobia.

"N—no," I faked a smile. "Just got a bit shocked, but I'm good." Ellie did not really buy it, but she did not ask any further. She looked up at the disappearing sun, then at me.

"Okay then, Lu," she removed her red and white cap, and placed it over my head. "Just let me know if you don't feel good." I nodded, and watched her walk toward Aiden, who also chose not to swim.

I focused on my Birks. I remembered calling them Jesus sandals. They were a gift from my mom's sister who had at least three pairs. My Birks had three black straps that wrapped around each foot. She gave Syd a pair, too, but his straps were beige, and five times bigger than my pair. I imagined Syd's big, beige Birkenstocks messily placed in front of his door, and I felt myself stop breathing.

Shaking my head, I felt the heat instead, and how better I would be if I just got over my intense dislike for water. I spotted Aerol close to the edge of the pool, playing cards with Aiden. He spotted me back, and motioned me to come over there. Taking a big sip of C2 and placing it inside my pocket, I cautiously walked toward the two. I ended up speedwalking as there was the white kid and his group of loud-mouthed friends going crazy with water guns and pool noodles. The water was going everywhere. I sat a few inches behind Aiden, waving to him and Aerol.

"How are you holding up?" Aerol somewhat knew of my dislike for the water. Heck, he knows a lot about me, and I'm honestly glad for that.

"Better than I imagined."

"You can't swim either?" Aiden looked relieved.

"Nope," I lied, but I guess this was one of those good lies because Aiden looked nine times happier knowing there was someone else who could not swim.

"I'd want to teach him but…" Aerol pointed at the noisy group of boys. My brows wrinkled at him.

"How was that basketball thing?" I asked Aiden. "How did you get out of it?"

"Ray was just about to assign me a position but then the talent show started," he shuffled the deck of cards." Hmmm, so his name was Ray.

"Would you like to play a good game of U—"

A line of water squirted out from Ray's water-gun, dead smack onto the deck of cards Aiden held. I gave the loudest screech.

"Ray!" I heard Ellie scream. She was marching toward us. Ray and his group of friends laughed like kings, loud and victorious. Aiden and Aerol looked at me more than the soaked Uno cards.

"Hey, hey, Lu," Aerol gestured at me to calm down. "Lu, it's okay."

My breathing was unstable. Ray's disgusting laughter clashed with Aerol's attempt to calm down. Above it all, I caught Dani in the far end of the pool. There she was, in her one piece, eyeing the situation. She caught me looking at her and she immediately turned around to face her friends.

"Boys, Lu, are you alright?" Ellie knelt down and placed her hand on Aiden's shoulder.

"Don't worry, Ms. Ellie," Aerol showed her a see-through Uno card. "Aiden brought the waterproof edition."

"Oh, that's a relief," she smiled. "And Lu?"

I froze. I feel like I was tied to a train track. The train's coming closer. I can't think straight. "Lu!" Too many distractions. Breathe in. Breathe out. I stared down at my Birks. "Lu!" Move! I pleaded. Move, you damn feet! Why don't you move?

"Lu—" I took a deep breath, willed my feet, and ran away from the pool before Ellie could say anything.

I closed my eyes, wanting to focus on just the wind hitting my face, the twigs I'm stepping on, and the small rocks that found their way into my sandals.

Bam! I bumped into someone. "Shit, sor—"

I looked at the familiar face. "Sayaka's friend, right?" Yukari took off her earphones. A smile appeared on her face upon realizing it was me, but soon faded into a frown.

"Yukari," she repeated in a monotone voice.

"Oh— I'm sorry...so sorry..." I apologized, flustered. She giggled.

"Come on, come on. I have to show you my dance," Yukari grabbed my wrist and dragged me through the patch of trees to a grassy spot. Her duffle bag rested on the trunk of a tree. She sat me down next to her bag before totally disconnecting her earphones.

"It's exciting," she placed her earphones back in their case. I crossed my legs, making myself comfortable for this small performance. She made sure her phone was at its loudest before placing it lightly in front of me, then she jogged back to the center.

Yukari began to dance the moment the song started. It sounded like a portal into a garden, filled with butterflies and bushes adorned with exotic flowers. Yukari's moves were magical, and something about her calm expression made the complicated dance look easy. She was light on her feet, hitting every move correctly with each beat. Her moves were filled with quiet self-confidence. She stayed in unmoving for three seconds after the song ended. I awoke from the trance and immediately applauded her, mesmerized at how she was able to memorize all that steps and not appear out of breath.

"Woah," was all I could say. "That was amazing." I handed her the face towel that peeked out of her duffle bag.

"Thanks," she wiped her face. "But I don't know if Sayaka would say the same."

"If who would?" We both jumped at Sayaka's sudden entrance.

"Sayaka," my eyes immediately went down to focus on her shoes. Her eyes were like that of a wolf.

"Why did you drag the short one here?" Sayaka pointed at me, asking Yukari in Japanese. Yukari rolled her eyes and bent down to grab her drink before walking away from the two of us. Sayaka bent down to look at me at eye level.

"She still needs practice, right?" She expected a 'yes' from me.

"I think she's pretty good already," Sayaka rolled her eyes at my answer.

"Oi, stop tormenting her, Saya," Yukari said in Japanese.

"How about you focus on your dance first?" Sayaka shot back.

"Not if you focus on your rap," Yukari fought back.

"Woah!" I stood up. The two girls glared at me. "Zero idea what you guys are saying. If you want me to leave, I can leave." Yukari and Sayaka whispered to each other before facing me.

"Watch us perform please," Yukari politely asked.

I looked at Sayaka then Yukari, "Okay, yeah, sure." I sat down next to Yukari's duffle bag, anticipating their performance. I waited for Yukari to give me a nod before I played the same music on her phone.

Once again. I was transported to that exotic garden of flowers and butterflies. I watched their dance styles contrast with each other, like autumn and spring. Sayaka's moves were sassy, keeping a light smile as her eyes lured you in. Yukari moved with ease, keeping a calm expression as she moved with accuracy and precision.

The song was a garden full of exotic flowers and butterflies, but these two were looking at two different bushes. For some reason, it felt like they were on the same book, yet on two different pages. I felt there was something wrong, but I could not really pinpoint what.

Once the song ended, they stayed in position for three seconds before standing up, dissatisfaction on their faces. They were mumbling to each other in Japanese, sounding both annoyed and disappointed at each other. I felt uncomfortable seeing them fight.

Pursing my lips, I had to think of something to distract them from their bickering. Usually, whenever Emmie and Alex would get into a pointless fight, Maya had this technique to calm them down. I hoped it would do the same to Sayaka and Yukari.

Quietly, I stood up and took a few steps to face them. It's now or never. Taking a deep breath, I recalled their dance moves, muttering the lyrics.

"Fiesta, na na na, na...mhm... hm hm hm hm..."

Sayaka and Yukari's bickering grew silent. They were speechless at my amazing dancing. The way I stretched my arms like a robot. The way I moved my feet like a baby who had never stood on its own two feet. I was spectacular. So spectacular that the two dancers burst out in laughter. It worked. Maya's strategy worked!

Yukari approached me, "Here, if you move your foot here, you'll get to the next move quicker."

Sayaka held my hand and fixed the position of my fingers, "Detail matters." The two girls looked at me, elated at teaching another soul.

"You want to give it another go?" Yukari asked. I nodded.

"Three, two, one, go!" Sayaka initiated. She hummed the chorus as Yukari kept an eye on me as I tried to apply whatever they taught me. At the end of the chorus, the two girls had smiles on their faces as they applauded me.

"You picked it up quickly," Yukari gave me a thumbs up.

"Quicker than Yukari," Sayaka said, receiving an eye roll from Yukari.

"But she reminds me of someone," Yukari's voice was softer when she spoke in Japanese. She whispered a name to Sayaka, who nodded as she pouted in agreement.

Yukari then turned to me, "Your dance reminded us of another camper, Dani," she translated. Sayaka agreed.

My smile instantly dropped. I looked up at the sky. Fortunately, the sun was setting. Without saying goodbye, I turned around and left the girls.

There were just too many trees. I cursed myself for not remembering my way back. I looked up and the corn blue sky slowly turned into a tad darker. I had to get back to the cabins.

That was when I noticed I was in front of the hill I saw this morning. I guessed this was a rather secluded area of the campsite. I could not hear noises coming from any camper, nor did I spot any sign of the mess hall or cabin anywhere. I would be sleeping on grass tonight, I guessed.

Curiosity got the best of me though, so I decided to walk up the hill. The tree looked way bigger up close and the hill was not that steep. It was not much trouble going up but still required abdomen power. Once I hit the top, I fell on my knees, exhausted but satisfied at my achievement. I then noticed a twitching silhouette. Someone was already up on this hill. Slowly, I stood up and walked to see the other side of the tree.

There was a person with a tablet on his lap. Man, I could not tell really. The figure was hooded and blended well with the slightly dim environment. Lightly, I tapped on his shoulder. He did not even look around.

"What bad thing did Ellie send you here for?" I jumped at how light the voice was. Her?

"Nothing," I sat down beside him, my legs close to my chest.

The view from the hill was pretty neat. There was a huge ocean before us, with mountains and trees to the side. I glanced at the person next to me, focused on his tablet. I sighed, lying down.

"You ever feel like Woody? You know, you've got your whole life together, it's all good and shit. But suddenly, Andy decides, 'Oh, I'm going to give you to someone who will definitely be happy to see you' and you're like 'But I'm already happy the way I am?' Then Andy's all 'I don't really give two shits about you, but I think you'll be better with Bonnie.' You know?" My arm draped over my face, covering my eyes. I heard a light chuckle.

"What's your name?"

"Lu," I replied. "Short for Lucy."

"Lu, huh?" the person snorted. "I'm going back to 505?"

I sprung up, "You heard it all the way here?"

"Yeah, mate," the person was too focused looking at his tablet. "Really strong voice. You in a band?"

"Probably not," I scratched my arm. "You?"

"I'm in a band, I guess," the person's finger slid up and down the screen. "Supposed to be me, Ells, and Barry. He's in Spain teaching soccer to kids. Ells doesn't want me to perform for the kids though. She's really worried about me being asked the feared question."

"Like what?" I chuckled to make it sound like my genuine question was a joke. "What are you?"

The person acted hurt, "Oh! Ooh!! There it is!!! The feared question!!" He started to laugh. "I'm human.

Isn't that obvious? I mean I wished I had wings, but eh, I guess I'll have to suck it up and walk on my feet instead."

I furrowed my eyebrows, trying to calm myself down. I asked a stupid question. Okay but what is a better thing to ask then? Then I remembered Ellie.

"What are your pronouns?" I asked. The person smiled.

"They/them," they replied. "Glad that Ells started a habit of asking."

I laughed nervously, letting the awkward silence do all the talking for the next few seconds. The person started to speak again.

"Questions like are you a girl? Are you a boy? What are you? Made Els really annoyed," they shrugged. "I mean all I have as a reply is 'I am a goat who likes making music!'" They gave out a small bleat, laughing. They nodded, "Never cared about genders and all that jazz. Nah, man. I'm into the infinite sounds and rhythms we can create."

"Music?" I perked up. They nodded.

"Yeah, man!" They offered their earbuds. Before saying yes, I glanced at their tablet and my expression fell immediately.

"Artificial music," I mumbled in disappointment. They slapped my back, laughing.

"Geez, man who taught you music?" They laughed. "Never in my life have I heard that. You're interesting." They inserted the earphones into my ears despite my reaction, wrapping their arm around me and swaying me side to side. "Music is music, fellow camper! It's a mix of melodies and rhythms and beats and anything your ears enjoy!"

I closed my eyes for a bit, pursing my lips then sighing. "Okay, fine. I'll listen." They began to press random buttons on the tablet. Oddly, it felt like the midnight blue of the night was filled with soft neon lights. It wasn't even a color that was a sore to your eyes. It was the combination of colors that soothed you while keeping you upbeat. I was thinking maybe reds, blues, yellows, and greens. It felt like I was in Times Square, where lights were everywhere and it felt so comforting in the midst of the loudness of the crowd. At least, I would not have to worry about monsters in the dark with all these lights protecting me. I was having a pretty good time until an annoying sound erupted out of nowhere, giving me a shock.

They said, "Sorry! It's my alarm!" I took off the earphones, cleaning the buds with my shirt before giving them back to them.

They continued, "Els is gonna kill me if she doesn't find me back at the cabins and sleepy Ellie is not someone you want to see." I watched them stand up. They smiled, patting my back.

"See you tomorrow perhaps!" Quickly, they began to go down the hill.

"Wait!" I shouted. They stopped in their tracks. "What's your name?"

"My name?" They shouted back, walking backward slowly.

"Hachi," I stared at my bowl of cereal. The name rang in my head after our encounter. Even after the next day, Hachi's voice still sounded as loud as ever in my mind.

"Oh, so you've met the goat?" Ellie paused from watching the camper next to her answer a math worksheet. The first activity of the day was Matema-kicks, which Aerol dragged me to go to. Ellie, who headed the program, was totally fine with me joining with no heads up.

"You were in a band?" I ate a spoonful of cereal. The activity was held at the mess hall, which was quiet in the mornings after breakfast when everyone was in their respective activities.

"Yeah!" Ellie smiled. "I mean, we still are." She nodded to the camper, signifying that his equation was correct before turning back to me. "Pretty rare for Hachi to be so comfortable around a camper they've just met."

I watched the milk drip from the spoon and back into the bowl. I wasn't thinking straight when I told her, "He makes artificial music—"

"They," Ellie was quick to correct.

"Sorry, they make artificial music," I swallowed another spoonful of cereal.

"Is that what it's called?" Ellie asked while still focused on the camper and his math homework.

"Hachi just told me it was music."

She then looked at me and shrugged, "Labels are pretty unnecessary, don't you think?"

I hummed as a response before swallowing another spoonful.

Ellie sighed, "I just wished they'd be confident enough to join me in watching all these kids." She opened her small lunchbox to bring out a container with apple slices and popped one into her mouth. "Or at least watch the showcase at the end of camp." She offered me a few slices.

"Showcase?" I took one apple slice and whispered a 'thank you'.

She nodded, "Yeah! Kinda like the talent show yesterday." I drank a glass of water to distract myself from yesterday's horrific event. Ellie seemed to be reminded and immediately added. "Bands can join! That is, if you don't want to go alone." She focused on the camper again.

The silence made me feel bad. Maybe I should have responded to her?

"Say," Ellie broke the silence again. "Why do you call it artificial music anyway? What's considered traditional music then?"

"Guitars, drums, bass," I listed the instruments. "Keyboards are borderline traditional and artificial." Ellie hummed in response.

"Do you like artificial music then?"

"Not really," I replied. "I used to play with this one girl before one of our bandmates died." I scratched my head, "Suddenly, we meet after a bunch of years, new band and all, and all of a sudden, her music is 99% confectioners' sugar and thrives on autotune."

Ellie laughed at my remark, "Maybe she likes the sound of confectioners' sugar and autotune in the same way you like guitars and drums." She smiled, "And, of course, the occasional keyboard."

"Maybe," I stood up to give my dishes to the ladies behind the food counter. I softly said Salamat Po as I handed them my empty bowl, spoon, and glass. They nodded and disappeared to the kitchen. I went back to my spot in front of Ellie.

"That's the beauty of humanities," Ellie closed the lid of her Tupperware container. "It's so diverse yet so connected."

It's so diverse it makes me sick, I thought.

"I'm sorry," the camper finally spoke. "I don't know how to do this."

"Oh," Ellie lightly took the worksheet from him. "Well, let's see. Hmmm…." She furrowed her eyebrows, struggling to understand the problem.

"May I?" Ellie nodded at my request, handing over the worksheet. "You just have to plug in 3 to x," I wrote down the equation. "Then once you've done that, you can simplify the denominator and numerator. Here, now you can find the solution." I handed the pencil and worksheet back to the camper, who looked astounded at how quick I understood the problem. Ellie had the same look of astonishment, she was impressed.

"Didn't know you were a math wiz, Lu."

"Lu's always had a thing for math," Aerol was walking toward us and overheard the conversation. "The only thing is, she doesn't want to show it."

I rolled my eyes. Ellie chuckled. Her phone sounded and she stood up immediately then turned to face the outside area. A muffled bell played through the PA system. "Okay campers!" She clapped loudly, "Put your math sheets into your folders and head to the forest! We'll be doing some destressing activities!"

The campers walked out of the mess hall either with their friends or alone. I stayed at the very back with Ellie and Aerol. The morning air was quite cold, but it wasn't so cold that you had to wear a jacket. You could survive just fine with a pair of shorts and a long-sleeved shirt.

"What's the next activity?" Aerol asked to break the silence. Well, not that it bothered any of us. Ellie was really absorbed in her phone such her eyebrows were furrowed and her thumbs moved at supersonic speed. Good luck to whoever's receiving her next message, I thought.

"Ugh," Ellie groaned. "Hachi bailed on me again." Aerol looked at me with concern.

"Sino?" Aerol whispered. I fastened my pace to keep up with Ellie, who started quickening her pace.

"Was Hachi supposed to take over our group?" I asked.

"Yeah," her eyes were glued onto her phone. "They promised me last night that this would be the day." She sighed and placed her phone back into her pocket, defeated. "Guess I can't always keep my expectations high."

"Is they always like this?" I felt a bit weird about the grammar, but I guess since we were only talking about Hachi, then the singular verb would go well with the singular noun.

"Only after they came out," Ellie wrapped her arm around me. She turned around and motioned Aerol to walk on her other side. "Hachi keeps on assuring me that they're fine being alone, but I don't know…" There was a look of sadness on her face, "Smiling doesn't feel right without them by my side." She realized what she had just said and laughed it off. "Cheesy, huh?"

"No, I don't think so," I replied. Ellie smiled and rubbed my shoulder.

"I just want them to be here," she opened up some more. "Not just up on that hill all day."

"The hill? You mean the Banshee of Bayanihan?" Ray crashed the conversation.

"Banshee?" I was disgusted by his incorrect nickname for Hachi. So many things were wrong with it.

"Yeah," he sounded smart for once. "Parents haven't been able to see their child after sending them to Bayanihan because of the monster." I looked at him, offended. Ellie snickered at his stupidity. Aerol noticed my glare and worried about what would happen next.

"Yo, Ray," he stepped forward to walk with the boy. "Tell me about your math homework." He wrapped his big arm around Ray's small frame. It looked like Aerol was about to choke him. The two walked away from me and Ellie. Thanks, Aerol, I thought.

"Boys," Ellie shook her head and laughed.

"At least name them a monster from Filipino mythology," I gave my thoughts, making Ellie laugh more.

"Totally agree," she smiled.

♪♪

We reached the spot where Sayaka and Yukari practiced. Obviously, the campers had never been here. They were amazed at the scenery, whispering that it gave them main-character vibes. Ellie called their attention.

"Okay, campers," she clasped her hands together, checking attendance with her eyes. "After a whole hour of using our brains to

solve math problems, I'm allotting this hour to explore our little forest here. Don't go too far away from here though." The campers nodded and began to walk around the forest with their friends.

I walked up to Ellie, pointing to the hill. She nodded before attending to two campers who wanted to show her the leaves they found. I felt a sense of relief seeing Hachi there in their natural habitat, headphones on and fingers tapping to a rhythm on their tablet. It reminded me so much of Sachiko. I felt a rush in my stomach thinking about my bandmates.

"Hey," I tapped on their shoulder to grab their attention. They nodded, giving me a smile before taking off their headphones completely.

"How's Bayanihan so far, Lu?"

"Fucking hell."

"Woah! Someone's not liking this place at all," Hachi dragged a light blue box on their tablet to the green box.

"No shit, Sherlock," I unconsciously remarked. Cupping my mouth immediately, I apologized. Hachi gave a comforting smile.

"Nah, don't sweat it," they pat my back. "Have you met your roommate yet?"

"Don't even get me started on the roommate," I covered my face. This whole camp was deemed bullshit. As much as I want to get out of this hell, it would only mean I have to face my mom and my bandmates.

The thought of going back to school and receiving the cold shoulder made my stomach churn. I moved my hands up to my hairline. I just could not go back. I could not. Even if I wanted to.

In my mind I saw Dani, eight years old. She was bawling her eyes out. Her words were mixed with short gasps and hiccups. "Lu…I don't want to be a part of this band anymore." I hated that face so much. Not that I liked seeing people cry, but it was the huge frown on her face, the way her tears left stains on her freckled face, her fists as she cried out of frustration and sadness. It was just her face I hated so much. I was the reason of that face.

I slowly let out a low groan as I ruffled my hair like a maniac, scratching my scalp with my long nails, creating new wounds on recently healed ones. I could not escape this. I really could not.

I felt a sharp object poke my side. I flinched, removing my hands from my face to see what had poked me. Hachi held out a small notepad and a pencil.

Their comforting smile and their little nudge for me to get the notepad and pencil brought me back to earth.

"Keep it if you must, Lu. I think Bernie will be a great friend of yours," they softly recommended. I swallowed, shyly taking the notepad and pencil.

"Now, tell me about your roommate," Hachi placed their tablet inside its black sleeve. "You two probably have history together."

I looked at them, "How do you know?"

Hachi shrugged, "A little bird named Ellie. She's a big fan of Breaking Daylights."

I did not really mind Ellie having an idea about my past, she probably needed it for records. Zero idea why they brought up Aiden's favorite band. Must've been famous.

"Did you have a disagreement or…?" Hachi asked. I lowered my head to focus on the grass we sat on, fiddling with them.

"Trick or treating seven years ago," I started. "A week after my brother died. We finished sorting and trading our candy. Me, her, and another friend of ours. Suddenly, she told me she didn't want to be part of our band anymore. My brother made a band and she was our bassist, but since he was dead, she thought this band wouldn't go on. So, what did she do? Moved to some new school, got dragged by a bunch of girls who are 99% confectioner's sugar and 1% human and then tell me she's part of some new band—"

Silence. I looked at them. I took a deep breath and continued.

"I got mad. She started crying."

They were quiet for a bit. "Were you really mad?" I was weirded out by the question.

"Well, of course I was. I mean— my brother made this band, wanted me, her, and that other friend to be part of it. He knew we had potential, music-wise. We would give rock a younger feel with our lyrics and our vibe, probably sell millions, break records, the whole shebang."

I checked if Hachi was getting bored of my fantasizing. They nodded for me to continue.

"But I was a dumb eight-year-old who hated change, even now," I looked at my nails. "Sucks I couldn't time travel so I could punch eight-year-old me in the face and tell Dani to do what she wanted with her musical abilities."

"So that's her name," Hachi realized. "No wonder she looks familiar."

"I have so much to tell her," I told them. "But I freaking hate one-on-ones." I pinched my nose. "I don't know…I just think of her and…flames of suppressed anger, fear, and…I don't know, sorriness? Is that a word? It just ignites in me, burns my organs, and my will to change. I end up just accepting reality: she hates me and there's really nothing I can do about it." They tapped their fingernail on the notepad, directing my attention to it.

"Suppressed anger, fear, and sorriness are always best conveyed through a chorus and a few verses," they smiled.

I looked at the notepad. Grabbing the pencil and twirling it a few times, I flipped to the first page and began to write a bunch of words.

Did you know that gravity pulls sideways
we don't have forever to debate
and love is not
like a game of cards, where
we both are fours, and you need an eight

Hachi was reading every single word I wrote, "Woah! You've got a way with words."

I shrugged, "They're just words."

Hachi gripped my shoulder, "And you've got complex emotions." We heard a distant bell coming from the mess hall.

They said, "Yo, you gotta go to your next activity. Ells might kill me if I keep you out for too long." We waved goodbye to each other as I walked down the hill.

12

The next activity was basketball. The counselor in charge of this activity was named Carlos and he looked like he stayed in the gym more than he stayed at home. He was buffed.

"Alright kids," he clapped his hands together. "We're playing a simple game of basketball today." Ray and his gang of jocks already began to plan out how the game's going to be played. Carlos seemed to be focusing more on the jocks than anyone else. He then glanced at everyone else, then back at the jocks, then back at everyone else.

"Who's the best at basketball here?" Carlos asked.

"Aiden!" Ray screamed as he raised his hand quickly. Aiden gave him a look of disbelief. Aerol and I sensed something wrong already.

"You're Aiden, right?" Carlos placed his humongous palm on Aiden's small shoulder. Aiden nodded, glancing toward me and Aerol and hoping we could get him out of this mess. I looked at Aerol, who looked even more concerned.

"Coach," Ray butted in. "Aiden's been playing ever since he was five. He's won a good number of trophies and even got personal lessons from Steph Curry."

"What the fudge!"

"Shh," Aerol stopped me from finishing my statement. It was so clear this little shit spat out nothing but lies. What makes more nonsense is that for some reason Carlos believed them.

"Oh, so he did," Carlos looked at Aiden with great expectation. "I'm not sure about your lessons with Steph Curry, but since you were five? Never knew I would be seeing a kid prodigy so soon!"

"Carlos," Aiden finally found his voice. "Ray's talking nonsense. I don't really play—"

"Coach! He's just being humble," Ray narrowed his eyes at Aiden. "He's just saying that because I'm here."

Carlos looked at the two boys before making a decision. "Okay, how about you two be captains and we'll have a little match? Choose your teammates."

"I'll be with Aiden," Aerol stood up from the steps. Carlos looked at him and motioned him to stay behind Aiden. Ray had no difficulty choosing his members. He chose his gang of jocks, who looked like they were the real ones who played with Steph Curry.

I've got to help Aiden out too. I thought. I could not help Dani because I was so full of myself. Maybe this time I could prove to her I've changed. Yeah, I smirked at myself, yeah this might be the climax of the story! Slowly, I stood up.

"I'll go with Aiden," Dani declared as she took her place behind Aiden. There was underlying anger in her voice. She obviously hated seeing all this go down.

"Good, red shirt," Carlos acknowledged Dani. He then looked at me, "You! Green shirt! Do you want to join?"

I opened my mouth to say something but no words came out. I even stuttered as I held onto the back of my head, grasping my hair tightly. I looked at Dani who shot dagger looks at me. I felt my self-esteem drop. It was crawling back into its comfort zone, crying for me to seek for Hachi.

I did not want to be here! I closed my eyes tightly. But if I leave, I thought, I'll be a pussy. No, I am not! This is being brave! Giving up is brave! Running away from things I can't handle is brave! Not choosing to play and running off to Hachi is brave! But... Aiden needs all the help he can get! But he's got Aerol... and Dani! But if I sit down, I might be called a wimp. If I run away to Hachi, I'll be sa—

Sayaka pulled my hand down, making me sit on the steps.

"They started playing already," she brought me back to reality. I sat down, embarrassed.

"Yukari's playing," she pointed to Yukari blocking one of Ray's jock friends who had the ball with him so Dani could steal it.

"She's pretty good," I remarked.

"If only she had this much body coordination when she danced," Sayaka laughed to herself. "Yukari has really good stamina. Even after hard games like these, she doesn't get tired. If I'm being honest, I wish I had that stamina." I looked at her.

"Did you two have a falling out?" I asked.

"Sounds very insignificant but," Sayaka hugged her knees closer to her. "Yukari was street-casted."

"Oh. "

She side-eyed me before continuing her story. "I had to wait for two whole months before I was accepted to the next round, then trained for four whole years after I got in, just to be told that I would be in a group with someone who only trained for three months."

It was hard for me to understand it completely. They were in an industry different from the ones I was familiar with, but I somewhat got her anger.

"It's unfair," Sayaka added.

"Must be," I said. "Don't you think Yukari feels the same amount of anger?" Sayaka glared at me. "Listen," I tried not to look at her eyes. "She's probably thinking she's damned to partner with someone who has been training for eons while she was just casted on the streets. She has to live up to your expectations. Think about it."

Sayaka did not say anything. She just hummed and continued to watch the basketball game.

"Dani!" A teammate shouted as he passed the ball to Dani. In a split second, she retrieved it and tossed it into the hoop with ease. Carlos blew the whistle as Aiden's team roared in victory.

Sayaka and I glanced at each other, unsure of whether to clap. We both awkwardly placed our hands down and smiled at the team savoring their win.

I watched Dani, the smallest of the team yet the MVP of the game, giving a high five to everyone, the biggest smile on her face. Aerol was too happy that he crouched and inserted his head between Dani's legs, making her scream as she was lifted up from the ground. I did not feel like looking anywhere else. I just wanted to savor her smile that turned her eyes into crescents and hid her freckles.

"I'll go to the toilet." I lied. I walked away from the court and into the forest.

13

Do you know the colors of the body?
They explain why I'm so drawn to you

I twirled my pencil as I stared at the words I wrote down with emptiness. Feeling the buttons of my shorts pushing at my stomach, I lifted the notepad and adjusted my position. I gazed at the water calmly flowing west. The area was a few meters away from Hachi's hill, but seeing that they weren't there, I decided to sit on this side of the forest, closer to the trees than to the body of water. I felt much better here. The sound of the water moving smoothly reminded me very well of why I was such a piece of shit in the first place.

The way the water flowed reminded me of the way Dani's tears fell smoothly off her cheeks. Her wails sounded like small drops of water crashing into each other. Loud enough for me to hear and recognize how painful my words were.

I wanted to comfort her. I wanted to pat her hair, and tell her it was okay. It was okay, Dani. It was okay, I was just a big idiot who should have died instead of my brother. You would have been a better sister than I had been.

My vision blurred. All I could see was a younger version of me, shouting all the curse words I could think of at an innocent Dani.

"Are you crazy? Kuya did not put you in this band just so you could get into some fake genre like pop! That's freaking stupid!" I cringed at the harsh words I threw at her.

"Lu, I don't want to play rock music! I like pop better!"

"Kuya saw talent in you! He pulled us all together! And you're just going to forget that and make Barbie music? You're a freaking joke, Dani."

My breathing grew unstable. I tugged my hair. The memory of Dani crying because of my uncontrolled emotions made me tug onto my hair even harder. Why was I like this? I lost everyone I wanted in my life. I was a freaking mess.

"Scream it out, Lu," Aerol's voice softly instructed me. With a deep inhale, I raised my head and screamed from my diaphragm. I heard a few birds escape the trees, and a kid from afar shouted "SHUT UP!" I burst into laughter, so did Aerol.

"Dani?" Aerol asked when we both calmed down.

"Yes. How did you know?"

"I've dealt with your tantrums since you were three," he walked toward the river and dipped his feet into the water. "You wore the same troubled expression when we went to your school to perform."

"Ha," I scoffed. "More like to replace us."

"Hey, we didn't know you were going to perform," Aerol replied.

"No, no," I shrieked. "It wasn't like my school never wanted to hear their own band play."

"Well, if it makes you feel better," Aerol lifted his feet out of the water, kicking them in the air to dry them off. "We were emailed a week before the performance. It was hell."

That did not make me feel better, you little shit. I felt my blood boil.

"We were emailed two fricking months before the performance. We spent our whole summer practicing." My hands trembled but dug at the earth with my nails. Aerol rushed up to me. He covered my hands with his.

"You're hurting the Earth, Lu—ser," Aerol told me.

I wasn't looking at him, "How about you shut up you freaking piece of sh—"

"You're just as reckless with words as Dani is," Aerol raised his voice and tightened his grip. He let them go when he saw me winced. "You both think for a long time yet somehow you end up saying all the wrong words." I looked up and saw his angry frown.

Silence.

I swallowed, "I'm sorry Aerol. I didn't mean to—"

Aerol did not even let me finish before he stood up and walked back to the campsite. I banged the back of my head against the tree that I rested on, covering my face with my hands.

"You just had to fuck up again, Lu."

I scolded myself mentally. I could just tone it down a bit. Yeah, as if that would work. I lifted my hand up to slap my face, but before I could swing my right hand, someone grabbed my wrist and slammed a rubbery pole on my palm. Aerol was back with a badminton racket!

"Chadminchon?" He asked. I could only smile at his endearing request.

"Psssh, sure," I stood up, placing the notepad inside my pocket. "Only if you're prepared to lose like… always?"

"Ready?" He waited for me to reach the other end of the field before positioning the neon yellow shuttlecock above his racket.

"Yeah," I twisted my wrist clockwise. It made a few cracks. I stared at my right hand, holding a racket after a lifetime. The last time I played badminton was when Syd was alive.

"Here we go," Aerol dropped the shuttlecock and hit the bottom part. His racket made a loud ping and created a high arc before landing at the perfect distance for me to hit it back with enough power.

Ping! "How's Dani in school?" I asked.

Pang! "Same as always," Aerol replied. "Class president, lowest grade is A minus, nothing new."

Ping!

Pang!

Ping! "Does she have any friends?"

Pang! "Carla and Martha."

Ping!

Pang! "They wanted me to be their manager—"

Ping!

Pang! "——once they thought of forming a band."

Ping! "How was she after the performance?"

Pang! "Not a word on our way back."

Ping! "She looked pretty happy on stage."

Pang! "Was she?"

Ping! "Why wouldn't she be happy?" I asked.

Pang! "Simple," Aerol replied.

Ping!

Pang! "Because that stage was meant for you."

The shuttlecock landed on Aerol's side of the field. One point for me.

"She looked so cool on the stage, honest," I picked up the shuttlecock then walked back to my spot. "Haven't seen her smile like that in a while." I held the shuttlecock above my racket.

"Dani thought the same thing about you," Aerol said.

I hit the shuttlecock and watched it land a few inches away from my feet. "Don't pull my leg," I sat in front of the shuttlecock, tired.

"Why? You think she'd hate you because you didn't want her to achieve her dreams because you didn't like the idea of her leaving you?"

I cringed at the accuracy.

"I've dealt with both of your crap since we were three," he walked closer to me. "I know you both. Too damn well."

"You really do," I nodded in acknowledgement.

"You can't be in a team together," he finally said.

"I know," I brought out my notepad and stared blankly at the words I wrote. "It's my fault for being so selfish."

"But you both need each other," he followed up. "Being a band wasn't the way though."

I did not know what he was implying. I still thought I was better off accepting the fact Dani moved on and wanted me out of her life as far away as possible.

"Stop."

♪♪

An eight-year-old Aerol held onto my shoulders tightly with his chubby fingers. I stopped shouting and for the first time, I felt fear. I was scared of this Aerol. This Aerol who knew he was the biggest one among the three of us and wasn't afraid to show it. He looked like he was about to dismember me.

I stayed silent as my legs started to weaken from fright. He did not say anything more once he let go of my shoulders.

Dani's wails softened to just soft hiccups as Aerol brought her out of the room, not wanting to turn back as he slammed the door hard and made me jolt.

Dani's soft hiccups became muffled but they were loud enough to echo endlessly in my mind.

♪♪

"Lu!" Aerol spun his racket up into the air and caught it. "We're still in the middle of a match, di ba?"

"Shit—yeah, yeah," I grabbed the shuttlecock and jogged back to my spot, feeling embarrassed for spacing out.

"Loser buys the winner Oreos?" Aerol suggested as he practiced his swing.

"Make it two packs," I bet with a smirk.

"Cocky now, are we?"

"No," I threw the shuttlecock in the air. "Just predicting the obvious."

Ping!

Pang!

Ping!

Pang!

Ping!

Pang!

Aerol made another huge arc, giving me time to move back two steps. My racket was open as my eyes stared at the white bottom of the shuttlecock. I reached out my left arm to the sky as I pushed my racket all the way to my back, my right elbow facing the sky. At the right time, I smashed the shuttlecock, watching it zoom over Aerol's head.

"Please—" Aerol shouted. He tried to drop low to try to make it in time before the shuttlecock hit the ground, but failed. The shuttlecock landed a few inches away from the tip of his racket. I screamed in joy automatically. I ran to the tree to grab the pencil that was just lying down in front of it.

"You win," Aerol grabbed the hem of his sleeve and used it as a towel to wipe off his sweat.

"Like always," I gloated.

"I owe you two packs of Oreos."

"That was the agreement."

"Golden and original?"

"Hasn't changed one bit," I confirmed.

"You two aren't as mad at each other as you both think, you know." I waited for Aerol to continue, but he walked back to grab the rackets and the shuttlecock.

"I'll go return these," he said. "Think about what I said."

"See ya at lunch," I waved.

"See ya," he said as he walked away. I listened to his footprints grow faint, until all I heard was the music coming from the noisy river.

I scanned the flow to the direction opposite Hachi's hill. The river seemed to drop down that way. Hmmm. There must be a small cliff at the far end. I got annoyed that the camp combined two my phobias—heights and water. So inconvenient.

I heard the bell from afar. My stomach growled in harmony, but I smiled as I thought of the golden and original Oreos that Aerol owed me.

The mess hall was full of sweaty teens munching on their chips and juices, kids with paint marks all over their arms as they talked about their new art pieces, and a long line of campers who seemed to have gotten used to waiting for their food. I rushed to one of the tables with empty chairs. My legs swayed as I excitedly waited for the Oreos that Aerol owed me. I looked at the long line of campers in front of me, hoping to find Aerol in the midst of everyone. I spotted Sayaka and Yukari at one table, feasting on fruits.

"Here is for winning the badminton match," my eyes widened at the sight of two glorious packs of golden and original Oreos.

"Don't mind if I d—"

Aerol snatched the two packs immediately and replaced it with a bowl of salad.

"This is for the multiple times you made Dani cry," he handed me a fork as he placed his own tray down next to my bowl. I groaned.

Ahhh, yes. Inside every angel is a nasty devil, I told myself.

"May I sit with you guys?" Aiden brought his tray with him. The two of us nodded and with a smile, he sat next to Aerol. I looked at what he was having for lunch.

"Spaghetti and fish fingers? Sounds pretty

delicious," I gave him a thumbs up. I then looked at my bowl of salad.

"Comfort food," Aiden smiled. He saw my bowl of salad and did not say anything.

"What do you think, Aerol?" I looked at him with a sinister smile. I could see him cringing.

"Why, is anything wrong?" Aiden asked worriedly.

"No, nothing," I snickered. "Aerol has this huge pet peeve with food touching each other when they aren't supposed to."

Aerol judged Aiden's plate, "No, no, it's nothing big, but I mean...just..." He took Aiden's fork and moved the fish fingers away from the excess spaghetti sauce. Aiden laughed.

Aerol smiled calmly and turned to me, "Now you." He pointed his lips to my salad. I closed my eyes tightly, not wanting to see the horrid visuals of the vegetables. "The longer you take, the longer it takes," he warned. I sighed.

"Fine, I'll eat it," I forked myself a piece of lettuce, staring at it with disgust. I took a deep breath and shoved a forkful of the salad into my mouth. I grabbed Aerol's arm to squeeze as I fought the urge to spit it out.

Aiden watched me squeeze Aerol's arm, "That looks pretty painful."

"Nah," Aerol calmly fed himself a spoonful of rice. "She's been like this ever since."

I sighed loudly, grabbing their attention, "I swallowed it!"

"Galing, Lu!" Aerol applauded. "Now five more then you'll be done!" I pressed my lips. This is straight-up torture.

"I don't see anything wrong with salads," Aiden said. "I mean, my dad was very strict with us, like we had to eat vegetables or we couldn't play outside."

"Yeah, but you see, Lu was different," Aerol talked about me as if I was a new type of specimen. "Lu just hates vegetables. Her mom didn't really force her to eat it. Lu was already playing badminton with me so it became my job, as her friend, to make sure she eats her daily serving of vegetables." He seemed proud, I had to give it to him.

"I enjoyed seven years without you telling me to eat the gulay in whatever soup we served," I grumbled as I quickly ate another forkful of salad.

"Pfft! Look where that led you," Aerol joked. I rolled my eyes.

"Don't listen to him, Lu," Aiden had my back. "You're very beautiful."

"Yeah, you really are," Dani joined the conversation.

I felt the salad stuck in my throat as I heard her voice. I began coughing, hiding my head under the table so she would not see me.

"Yo, Lu! Are you okay?" Aerol patted my back, handing me a glass of water.

"I'll sit here," Dani sat in front of Aerol, placing her tray on the table, ignoring my coughing.

I could not spit out the food on the floor so I grabbed the glass of water from Aerol and chugged it down. Facing the ceiling, I managed to swallow the last forkful of salad and sighed loudly.

"You're 15 and you can't eat vegetables? You can't live on milk and cookies that long, Lu," Dani tried to joke. "You aren't Santa."

I looked at her quickly, then looked somewhere else. I could not even look her in the eyes for five seconds.

"Not all 15-year-olds can eat vegetables," I muttered like a baby. I walked out of the mess hall without eating my prized Oreos.

15

I stayed in the cabin until it was around evening, when the lights were off. Despite being roommates, I did not bother lifting my head up from the bed to check if Dani entered or not. It felt good to have a reason to be mad at her, even if she did have a point with her words. I just did not want to admit it.

I checked outside the window to see the night sky. It was probably around 1 am. I sat up to check if Dani was still sleeping.

Oddly the bed was flat. Her clothes were tidied into her luggage. I got out of bed and crept toward hers. The bed was neatly made, as if no one slept here in the first place. Something about this did not sit well with me. I found a piece of paper. Crumpled.

"Going for a swim. Join if you want."

I froze. The paper fell to the floor. My heart was beating fast, my brain tried to calm it down, I was in a panic. Too many thoughts appeared at the same time, racing through my brain like cars trying to get into first place.

I could not think straight, but I knew time was slipping away. I did not bother grabbing a pair of shoes as I rushed out of the cabins. I reached the pool breathless. There wasn't enough time for me to catch my breath. She wasn't in the pool.

"No, no, no, no..."

I ran to the river past Hachi's hill. My head moved from side to side quickly as I looked for Dani. I could not find her. I speedwalked to the edge of the river.

There she was. Passing by me. Lifeless.

I jumped straight into the water, paddling my way toward her.

"Dani!" I screamed, diving underneath so I could lift her body. I brought my head up and saw that we were almost near the edge of the cliff.

I grabbed her shoulders, led her quickly to the riverbank, and lifted her heavy body up from the water. I threw her upper body onto the grass. I pulled myself up and dragged her far from the river. I saw one of her slippers detach float down toward the edge of the river. I was too tired and scared to even worry about retrieving it.

Once Dani's whole body was on the grass, I collapsed trying to hold in my screams. I was still catching my breath as I checked on Dani.

"Dani, wake up." I grabbed her wrist to feel a pulse.

I could not stop myself from panicking. I had no idea how to check if she was alive or not. I did not read enough books to prepare myself for this. Maybe I should have taken Aerol's advice and read more books instead of watching TV.

Memories came rushing in. I could see my mom's face when she saw Syd's lifeless body on the bathroom floor. "Syd! Syd!" She cried in desperation and said nothing after that. Still shaking, Mom bent her head and whispered prayers.

As an eight-year-old, I asked myself why she had to pray. At fifteen, I did the same thing. I closed my eyes tight and I intertwined my fingers together, trying to stop my brain from jumping to conclusions.

"Please," I whispered. "Don't take her, too." It was stupid, I know. I could've just dragged her to Ellie and Hachi. They would have known what to do. But I was still trying to calm myself after jumping into the water. My legs felt numb. Then Dani started coughing.

"Holy shit," I blurted. Gently, I lifted her head up.

Dani slowly opened her eyes and saw me. She did not look one bit relieved. She pushed me away with all her might and stood up, still shaking but regaining her balance. From the ground, I gave her a look of shock at the audacity of her response. She gave me one last look before stepping away. I stood up and chased her.

"Hey, what got into you?" I was mad. Like a mom who just witnessed her child made a whole mess of her room.

"Shut up, you moron," Dani growled. "At least your mom actually cared about you."

I stopped in my tracks at her stupid assumption. She cussed harshly, too. I rebutted, "My mom gave zero shits about what I wanted to do and placed me in this damn camp without telling me. You think that is caring?"

Dani turned around, "Maybe if you weren't so caught up in trying to chase after Syd, you'd see how much your mom cares!" She screamed at the top of her lungs.

"Hah!" I laughed sarcastically. "You really did become some artificial bitch after leaving Syd's ba—"

"Syd is fucking dead!"

Her fists remained tightly clenched as she stomped toward me, making me walk back in fear. There was silence. She licked her lips and continued.

"Syd's freaking dead! You think you should've died instead of him, maybe you should! It's always you! I'm freaking sick of you being the reason your mom smiles while I'm freaking rotting here being nothing more than a tool for my mom!"

She breathed heavily. Her eyes locked on me. They were still hungry. They weren't satisfied yet.

She pointed to herself, "My mom never gave a damn about me— She just used me to compete with your mom!" She stomped her feet like a toddler.

"Dani—" I reached my hand out to her. Like a wild animal, she stepped back, eyes still filled with bloodlust. She wasn't done yet.

"None of this would've happened if Syd hadn't died, or if your mom just freaking knew how much my shitty mom idolizes her!"

Dani's voice began to crack, "It makes me question if being alive is even worth it!" Tears were falling down her wet face, dropping in sync with the water droplets from her hair.

"Go fuck yourself, Lu," Dani wiped her tears, looking vengeful. "All you think about is your brother. Look around, you piece of shit." She sighed, glaring at me one more time.

"Do your brother a favor and kill yourself," she spoke with undisguised hurt as she turned around with no thought of waiting for me.

My heart was racing. Never in my life have I heard Dani curse. I froze as I watched her figure grew smaller and smaller. My legs were already too tired to move another step. I collapsed to the ground. There were tears dropping to my damp pajama pants, I shivered some more.

I was transported back to the practice room, amidst the thrown bags, plastic chairs and tables, with an angry Alex in front of me, Maya's whimpering to fill the silence, "You and Syd were so close. We weren't even near the word almost." I heard Alex in my head. She was right. So was Dani.

Syd was dead. I knew that very well as I dug my fingers into the earth.

"I know he is dead," I muttered.

I stopped. Did I just acknowledge that he was physically gone? That he was dead?

I did. But I was still alive, so was Dani. And Aerol.

I relaxed my hand and raised my head, and rushed out to catch Dani.

♪♪

I returned to our cabin. Shivering from the cold wind, I grabbed the door knob only to find out it was locked.

"Uh…Dani???" I knocked on the door. "Could you…um…open the door? It's pretty cold outside." I sniffed the dripping mucus back into my nose.

The door opened but it was too narrow I could only see Dani's one eye. "You're staying outside, dumbass."

"Wait—"

The door slammed shut before I could protest. I gave a loud sigh, hoping she heard it. This was why I should never try to push Dani past her limits. She could turn into a demonic spawn raised from hell.

Fighting against her would not do me any good so I leaned and slid down the door, hugging my knees as tight as I could to keep myself warm.

"Could I at least have a blanket and a pillow?" I shouted. The door opened and Dani threw out her used towel and her wet slipper before slamming it shut again.

Honestly, I could have kicked the damn door, or entered the window, or ran to alert Ellie, but I chose to stay put.

"I could've kicked the door," I repeated to myself aloud as I moved away from the door. "I could've entered the window." I placed the slipper underneath my head as I laid down. "I mean, I could still run to Ellie's place. Maybe shower there instead," I imagined the hot water hitting my skin as I placed the towel over my damp body.

So why, Lu? Why were you staying here?

Even if I had the chance to get Dani in trouble, I felt like there was a reason all this was happening. I mean, this was supposed to be some wild chapter in my young life. It would be pretty exciting to tell everyone about the time I got kicked out of my cabin and was given only a slipper and towel to sleep on.

I yawned and felt a chill ran up my spine. I curled up into a ball and forced my eyes shut. Slowly my body relaxed at the sound of the birds chirping. My last thought was of Dani.

♪♪

One afternoon, Syd was being falsely accused of smoking after returning from a friend's party. It was from this photo of him holding a pack of cigarettes on one hand and a burning cigarette in another. Mom was fuming with anger and spitting questions left and right. Syd stayed silent, listening to every word of indignation spouting out of Mom's mouth, holding on to his guitar tightly.

After the outburst, Mom left me and Syd in his room to calm down. Syd told me the truth: He caught his friend smoking and he managed to convince him to stop immediately. He held the cigarette box and cigarette, but did not know someone was taking a photo of him at that moment. He threw the box in the trash can. I asked him why he never told Mom that when she was in the room.

"It was understandable that she'd get mad. What if you saw Dani take a photo with Petite Calvary?"

"I would freak out," I answered without thinking. "I thought she hated that group. I would think that she was keeping a secret from me."

"Exactly what happened to Mom," Syd placed his guitar on his bed. "It's a basic lesson in this house, di ba? Never talk to mom when she's mad because her voice will override your side of the story. You always have to wait for her to calm down to tell her."

I nodded.

"But of course, being silent isn't always the answer. Sometimes you really have to shove it in their faces," Syd laughed. He extended his arms and wrapped me tightly in them. The smell of cedar wood has never been so strong.

16

I felt like shit. My head was spinning. I was sweating and shivering at the same time and had no idea whether I was cold or not. My body was too tired to even open the blanket. I was paralyzed.

There was something wet and cold on my forehead. Reacting to it, I slowly opened my eyes to see Ellie's concerned face.

"Lu, go back to sleep," she sounded like my mom. She hovered her hand over my eyes and closed them. I took a deep breath and went back to sleep.

I slept for probably an hour before I felt strong enough to open my eyes. I noticed the silence in the room and thought no one was inside. I lifted my upper torso and rested on my elbows to examine the room. Dani was reading a book, not changing her uninterested expression as she turned to face me. She said nothing before going back to her book, turning a page.

"How was last night?" She asked monotonously.

"Ah, splendid," I said weakly.

"Apparently you can get grounded in camp," she turned to another page as her tone sounded really annoyed. "Didn't know my mom hacked the rules." I rolled my eyes as I heard her sigh.

"And now I'm stuck here with you." We said the same thing with the same level of annoyance and indifference.

We looked at each other, wide-eyed. I crashed my head back into my pillow. We were quiet for a bit.

"Play me something, boy," my voice was raspy. "You have a guitar with you yeah?"

Dani said nothing as she dragged the black guitar case out from under her bed and hauled it to mine. She placed the guitar on her lap as she leaned against the wall. I turned to my side so I could see her play the guitar. My eyes then went to her guitar case. I saw a keychain of a yellow blob with a winking face.

"You still have Mr. Pudding?" I pointed to the blob. She detached it from her guitar strap so I could get a better look at it.

"You probably lost yours," Dani mumbled as she tied Mr. Pudding back. "What do you want me to play?" She asked in a louder voice.

"Bahay Kubo," I said.

Dani gave me an odd look, "You're kidding me."

"I always sing Bahay Kubo when I'm gloomy."

"Seriously?"

Ba...

I started singing, waiting for Dani to start strumming. Once I heard the C chord, I continued.

...hay kubo kahit munti. Ang halaman doon

"Dani, sing for me. My throat hurts," I pretended. Dani groaned, but did not show any sign of annoyance as she sang.

Singkamas at talong, sigarilyas at mani…

I joined in.

Sitaw, bataw, patani

Dani eased up a bit on her strumming.

Kundol, patola
Utot, kalabasa

I sang seriously. Dani stopped playing as she cupped her face in her palms. I could hear muffled laughter.

"Why what's wrong? Is my voice really that bad?" I asked. No response. "Uy, uy," I poked her, slowly breaking into a smile as I heard her laugh louder. "Why did you stop?"

"It's been years since I heard that joke," Dani tried to calm herself down by exhaling deeply. "Agh, I thought I was mature enough to not laugh at that."

I smiled at her. "It means you have great humor." She looked at me with happy tears.

I continued, "Never underestimate yourself. The kids seen as immature make better songs than the ones who think they are mature."

Dani sounded interested, "Really?"

"Yeah," I told her. "Great singers would crack up at fart jokes that would slip out of someone else's mouth."

"Do they though?" The smile never left her face.

"I mean, you did," I received a slap from Dani. I watched her stand up, placing the guitar down on the floor crossing her arms.

"Our bands are enemies Lu," she recalled. "You're traditional, and I'm artificial."

I was taken aback, "Since when did you think that?"

"Ever since you told Ellie," Dani mumbled again, fidgeting with her fingers. My heart sank down to my stomach.

I sat up and faced her, "Throughout the camp, I've been visiting that hill near the river." I checked to see if she was still listening. "And, uhmm, I met this person who found comfort in the sounds of the city mixed with slow beats, everything's made on their laptop. Like, they push buttons to make unique sounds and catchy rhythms that sound so ethereal I couldn't imagine them being played on any normal instrument." I scratched my head before continuing.

"Made me realize just how much music really evolved, and how it just continues to evolve and evolve." I took a deep breath and tried to look at Dani's eyes, but I looked away immediately.

"Look, I take back what I said about your band being artificial. Music played through a synthesizer is just as good as music being played on a guitar. I think having both instruments creating music in harmony could result in even better music." I closed my eyes and waited for her next move.

I felt a sudden weight on my bed. I opened my eyes to see Dani sitting on the edge of my bed.

"Your band could use a synthesizer," she suggested. "I feel sad seeing you stuck in the Maxxed Out mold."

"Mmm, I like the Maxxed Out mold," I shrugged. "But I think my members might go for a new mold."

Dani chuckled.

"What happened to us, Lu?"

I removed the damp towel from my forehead, quietly placing it on my bed frame.

"We were so much better before," she watched me lightly tap my cold forehead.

"I think we're better off this way," I placed three fingers on my forehead to confirm it was indeed cold. Dani looked offended. "We're making music we like, right?" I followed up, "And we're enjoying it."

"Yeah," Dani agreed. "I guess I am enjoying making pop songs and performing with the girls." She looked at me again, "You aren't pissed we aren't performing together like when we were kids?"

I shook my head and put on a happy smirk. "I know how we can perform together one last time."

17

Bayanihan End-of-Camp Party—Band Sign-Ups
Aerol, Lu, Dani

It was almost impossible to remove the smile off Dani's face after Aerol finished writing down all our names.

"We're back for a proper goodbye," I channeled my inner hero character, feeling the chills as I said what was probably my coolest line yet. Dani relaxed her shoulders and nodded in agreement.

"I'm glad you remembered this, Lu," she could not take her eyes off our names on the sign-up sheets. We stared at them for a bit longer.

Aerol turned to us. "I haven't played in a while, but—I mean—a few sessions could help me loosen up."

"I'm pretty okay with playing the bass," Dani sounded confident with her answer. They both looked at me, waiting for my answer. I opened the collar of my shirt for a bit of air, nervously laughing.

"Ahh...actually...could I not do the guitar? Just for this! I can do— maybe the drums? Syd gave me like two lessons on it, but I know the basics!" I wanted to convince them. They did not buy it. I sighed in defeat, dragging myself to the steps a few inches away from the sign-up sheets. Aerol and Dani sat on each side of me.

"Come on, Lu," Aerol rubbed my back, "Arctic Monkeys may not have been your forte, but this is a perfect opportunity to show off your guitar skills!"

I forced a smile, "Thanks...but...I really think someone else should play the guitar for me—"

"You need another guitar player?" Aiden's sudden appearance startled us.

"Uhhh, yeah!" Aerol felt quite relieved to see Aiden, "you know a few chords?"

"Mmmm... not on the guitar, but would a uke work?" Aiden unzipped a bag he had been carrying to showcase a uke with a gazillion fishes on it. The design definitely shocked us. But it did not stop there. Aiden took us in for another shock. He began to pluck the strings in a melody that was rather nostalgic. Judging from the quick glances Aerol gave at me, there was something about this nostalgic melody that I did not know about.

I brushed him off, too mesmerized at Aiden's graceful plucking to give Aerol a care. My eyes darted from Aiden's fingers to his face, controlling his satisfied smile.

By the time he was done, the three of us immediately stood up. Aiden held his uke by the neck and waited for our answer.

No words were needed. Aerol rushed to the sign-up sheets to write a name while Dani and I watched him finally break out into a big grin. Dani, Aiden, and I then walked up to Aerol and admired our names.

Aerol, Lu, Dani, Aiden

"Let's practice now!" I smiled at each one of them.

Hear Me Out

♪♪

Hachi introduced us to their small shed where they stored most of their music instruments. They called it Hachi's Habitat, but because it was so stuffy, they spent most of their time on the hill. Ellie, too, was okay with us staying far from the campus, as Hachi was there to keep an eye on us.

We started off by thinking of possible songs to sing. Everyone wanted their song to be chosen.

"Prom Queen by Beach Bunny!" Dani hoped someone would agree with her.

"I was thinking more of Juicebox by The Strokes," I shot back.

Aerol clapped his hands and declared, "Girls, you do know your tastes in music are completely different." We both nodded. "I say we go safe and roll with some Simon and Garfunkel? Like Mrs. Robinson?"

Dani and I mouthed "No" as we shook our head.

"I think we'd need something more...upbeat," I suggested. Dani and Aerol nodded in agreement.

We were allowed to perform once so the song choice should be something that accommodated all of us. There was silence as each member thought long and hard. I imagined everyone mentally scrolling through their playlists.

Mine was a mix of Strokes, and a bit of Artic Monkeys and Phoenix. Dani's was probably full of Cavetown, Beach Bunny, and Tessa Violet. Aerol's got Bob Dylan, The Beatles, and a few tracks of Frank

Ocean in there to be hip with the kids. I did not know about Aiden's list.

I turned to Aiden, who was stroking the little fishes on the smooth wood of his uke.

"Aiden, do you have any suggestions?" It was my turn to make him jump.

"Uhmm, well...there's this song I heard."

18

"Before you left Zoe to be beaten up by your own classmates?"

Raymond appeared with a smirk on his face like Doofenshmirtz every time he succeeded in trapping Perry the Platypus. We all turned to watch him casually walk up to us. "My despicable classmate Aiden. How could you do such a thing?"

His voice sounded so fake the sun could melt the plastic off him. I kept my eyes on him. His cocky ass approached us with such confidence that it made me angry. From the corner of my eye, Dani was keeping her eyes on Aiden. Aerol stood up from his seat and looked down on Raymond.

"Do you need anything?" He asked.

Raymond narrowed his eyes at him, "Nothing much. Just that asshole who's missing out on a good game of basketball."

Aiden clung to his uke, not wanting to look at the smaller boy. "Raymond," his voice was shaky already, "I told you I don't play basketba—"

"Oh, enough with the bullshit!" Raymond was angry.

Aiden, as if on reflex, turned around and looked at him in utter fear. His muscles tensed up and his shoulders raised up. Dani rushed to his side. I stood up, too, not wanting to get my eyes off the little shit named Raymond. We all waited for what he had to say.

"You left WSC so no one could beat you up about your thing with Zoe," Raymond pointed his finger at Aiden, making the other boy shake. "Don't think that by leaving one school, you're considered clean. The girls at my class are freaking ruthless when it comes to betrayers like you."

As much as my heart was beating, something didn't make sense. I turned back to see Aiden's face. He stopped shaking, but there was an underlying anger inside him that he controlled, just like his smile.

"How could you be so worked up over Marcus?" Aiden finally spoke. His voice so low to keep it from shaking. Everyone made sure to stay silent so we could hear him clearly. "Marcus had no friends."

"Marcus had none," Raymond interrupted. "Zoe did."

"I would like it if you called him Marcus," Aiden was firm.

"Why? You're unwilling to accept the fact she's a girl?" Raymond laughed, "She tried to get close to you by being a boy. Don't you get it? You were played."

"That was never the reason that Marcus transitioned," Aiden gripped onto his uke tighter.

"Well, that was the reason that reached Alyssa," Raymond shrugged his shoulders. "That was the reason that reached everyone."

"That still doesn't mean he's going to play basketball with you," Dani spoke. Raymond glared at her before smirking.

"Alright then, smart one," he placed his hands on his hips. "What if I told you that Aiden began skipping basketball practice just to stay with Zoe then? He was one of our best players. Seems like he was so good, practice was nothing but bullshit."

"I don't see why you're so into Aiden's life," Aerol pursed his lips. That was the sign he was about to snap.

I remained silent, unsure of when to step in. The story was still unclear to me, and the fact the conversation moved quicker than my mind could process made my heart beat faster.

"Oh, you want to know why? I liked Alyssa. Yeah. Truth's out! I liked Alyssa!" Raymond placed his hands up in surrender. "But you know who Alyssa liked? Aiden. And who did Aiden like? Alyssa's best friend, Zoe. Every single day, it was 'Zoe this' and 'Zoe that.' I couldn't stand seeing her this angry and pissed at someone who was long freaking gone!"

I watched the veins on his neck bulging. He took deep breaths to think of his next few sentences. "All she talked about was Zoe, even after she became known as Marcus. Alyssa never wanted to accept it. Just the damn fact that you were there, so oblivious to everything that was happening was infuriating."

Raymond's voice softened, "But now that you're gone, and Zoe's gone, Alyssa's not the same anymore. No, she isn't." His laugh was creepy, but he stopped as soon as he saw Aiden tightly gripping his ukulele. Angrily, he walked toward Aiden.

Raymond continued, "It's all shit. Alyssa meant so much to me. She never knew it. Every tear, every rant, every sigh was all because of you and Zoe. You don't know how I felt." His face was turning red. "All I could do was sit back and watch Alyssa destroy herself, Zoe leaving the school, and you quitting the basketball team—"

I gripped Raymond's wrist before he could snatch Aiden's uke, my nails digging into his pale skin.

"Raymond, listen to me," I tightened my grip whenever he squirmed, "She's stuck in the past, but you aren't. Alyssa doesn't deserve you. Wake up, and move on." I tried to smile, "Trust me, Raymond. I know how it's like to watch change happen in front of you and not being able to do anything." Raymond looked at me. His wrist relaxed and I let him go.

"You really think a freaking lesbian like you would understand how I feel? Go hit four eyes over there," he cocked his head toward Dani, who could not believe what she heard. My face grew warm.

"Quite some nerve for someone who couldn't even assert himself. You fudge off!"

"Woah!" Aerol and Dani growled at the same time, big smiles on their faces. Raymond checked everyone but was not about to let go of what he wanted to do in the first place.

"Just let me have the damn basketball player and we don't have to talk ever again."

"Yeah, sure! Right after forcing Aiden to pla—"

"I asked him to join. He said yes. He's just saying no now because—"

"You asked him, my ass!" My heart was like Maya playing on her drums whenever she came to practice annoyed. Just unrhythmic banging, trying to pop out of my chest. "You literally grabbed him then without any warning!" The drums in my chest banged louder as I shouted. Raymond was not one bit guilty of his actions.

"Look, I don't see any problem. He clearly wasn't complaining when we played," Raymond pointed to Aiden.

"It's because you didn't use your freaking ears," I cocked my head.

"What is it to you? Just let me have Aiden."

I licked my snaggletooth and gripped his right hand in one fluid stroke, "Since you have the habit of not listening—"

Raymond did not know what hit him as I folded my arm and drove my elbow to his chest. As his upper body curled over, my left fist connected with his chin.

"Woah!" I heard my bandmates screamed in delight.

"You're freaking stupid, Raymond." He placed his hands on his chest as he backed up. His breath was shaking. He finally hit a tree and jumped a bit upon feeling the trunk on his back. The cocky smile never left my face as I stared at him, ready to pounce again. He stumbled on his feet as he raced back to the basketball court. Victorious, I turned around with open arms to my bandmates.

"Lu, may I hug you?" Aiden was on the verge of crying.

"Sure!" I replied, delighted. He then wrapped his arms around me and gave me a tight squeeze before turning it into a warm embrace. I rested my chin on his shoulder and smiled as I patted his back.

"It never felt the same once Marcus left," Aiden sniffed. Dani smiled at me. "I owe you one."

Aerol ruffled my hair once Aiden let go of me. "Let's practice!"

"Marcus was a really cool guy," Aiden tuned his uke once more before handing it to me. "If it wasn't for him, I wouldn't have learned the uke."

"Did you know him before he transitioned?" Aerol asked. Aiden shook his head.

"Apparently, Alyssa did. Marcus told me that it was all a misunderstanding between him and her."

"How about you and Raymond?"

"Yeah, how did his stupid ass get into this story?" I smirked as I handed him the guitar. Aiden positioned the guitar on his lap.

"We were both on the basketball team. He was a benchwarmer and I was one of the only seventh graders to become a main player on the team." He plucked a few strings to hear each different note. "I remember Raymond being a pretty energetic kid, especially with his older brother who was captain around that time. I would see him run up to him with sparkly eyes, only to see him get sent to the benches. Pretty sad to see, really. I also heard around that time he had a thing for Alyssa, who was also equally upbeat. Those two hang out a lot together. Marcus came in at the start of eighth grade. Rumors hounded him, most coming from Alyssa herself."

Hearing about Raymond and his brother made me feel a bit bad for snapping at him. Syd was never the kind to dismiss me, but I, too, would have been angry if I was treated the same way. Then again, I only feel just a bit bad.

"I spotted Marcus playing the uke one day in the gym alone. I was supposed to pick up my water bottle I left the day before, but there was something about his playing that drew me in like the Pied Piper. I was hooked. I asked him all about the uke; he answered every question with his little smile that showed his snaggletooth. Man, that smile …" Aiden caught himself smiling and covered his mouth. I gave him a warm smile back while Dani was giggling. Aerol nodded, waiting for him to continue.

"So, I went up to the gym to practice on Mondays and Wednesdays, then the remaining days were spent playing the uke with Marcus," Aiden pretended to strum the guitar, making the sounds through his mouth instead.

After a light laugh, Aerol fell silent. "Well, it was Thursday. I didn't see any sign of Marcus when I went to class. Our rooms were right across from each other. I found his seat empty. I thought it was just bad timing whenever I peeked, so I went to ask his teacher personally. All he said was that he was absent,'" Aiden paused.

"I entered the classroom around dismissal, and opened the huge cabinet every classroom had out of curiosity. I saw his uke there. Smashed into bits. Really, really dumb words were written all over it…" He fell silent once again.

We did not pressure him to continue. Instead, we all lowered our heads to ponder on his story and its loopholes. The silence lingered for a few more seconds before Aiden continued.

"It's— uhm—pretty sad story, but don't worry. Marcus gave me one of his spare ukes as a gift, personally doodled like his! We both moved to different schools and I think it was for the better." He shook his hands to signal to us that we need not worry.

"The teacher should've done something about it," Dani spoke up. "Did he know about it?"

"Or did Raymond manipulate him with his victim shit?" I leaned forward to Dani.

"He probably knew about the whole thing and didn't want to just tell Aiden what happened out in the open," Aerol was always the one who looked at the reality of things. Dani and I turned to Aiden, wondering if any of our answers were correct. Aiden just smiled.

"Well, actually…" Aiden lingered on his words. The three of us leaned in, wondering what this teacher's real identity was. Was he an ally in Aiden's story? Or was he a traitor?

Aiden continued, "The teacher's backstory will be revealed…" He looked at each one of us, "After the break!"

"Damnit, Aiden!" Aerol groaned. Dani, Aiden, and I burst into laughter seeing Aerol so annoyed.

"That story's something between me, Alyssa, Marcus, Raymond, our parents, and the teacher," Aiden placed his finger in front of his mouth.

"Oh," Aerol understood but he was still annoyed.

A loud sigh escaped Dani's mouth, "What song did Marcus love?"

Aiden rested his chin on his palm, fingers touching his cupid's bow as he thought hard, "Well, he did like You Know It by Colony House."

Aerol, Dani, and I all looked at each other once again. Smiles on our faces. I turned to Aiden, "What are the chords?"

20

"Inhale." Haaaaa!

"Exhale." Huuuuu!

"Remember, no one enjoys a stiff performance. and, imagine everyone is naked."

"That's gross!" I reacted to Syd's advice, my face turned red from embarrassment and feigned anger. He laughed as he ruffled my hair, which actually made me angry. Mom spent a whole hour fixing my hair just for him to mess it up.

"Fine. How about you imagine everyone is Mr. Pudding?" Syd's suggestion put a bright smile on my face.

"Mr. Pudding! Like the keychain I and Dani have!" I showed him my incomplete set of teeth when I smiled. Syd nodded. He knelt down and placed his hands on my shoulders.

"Your passion is like a bunch of exploding stars. It's such a sight to see Lu! So, let's kill this."

I had no idea what he meant by this, but it came from Syd so I suppose it meant something good.

"Okay."

"Breath in, breath out, Lu."

Syd stood up and got ready to go up the stage.

♪♪

"Everyone is Mr. Pudding," I repeated to myself in a whisper.

I retreated to the hill two hours before the big performance. I wanted Syd to sit down next to me. I wanted to tell him his technique for removing nervousness was a scam.

Every exhale left me more anxious than the last, each breath becomes shakier. Eventually, I let out one big sigh and lifted my head to look at the slowly darkening sky. The moon would be majestic tonight.

La Luna. Syd enjoyed writing that word a lot. He used it a lot when he would write songs or essays for school. I hope he was chilling on the moon. I squinted my eyes, as if that could make me see him better.

"The moon's such a beauty," Hachi spoke.

"Yeah…" I mumbled. Closing my eyes, I tried to do a few more breathing exercises.

"Scared?" Hachi asked. I nodded.

"A bit," I opened my eyes to adjust the strap of Aiden's uke. "But…I kinda like this feeling."

Hachi stretched their mouth and let out a hearty laugh, "You're really something Lu." They proceeded to pat my back so hard I leaned forward.

"I'm being real!" I defended myself while laughing. "The last time I played on stage was when my brother was still here." My voice slowly lowered upon remembering my first performance. "Probably wasn't feeling this anxious back then but damn these butterflies! They're more like moths around a light, fluttering nonstop."

"Syd, right?" Hachi recalled as they looked up at the night sky. The stars were beginning to get more and more visible the more we stared at them.

"Yeah," I brought my legs up to my chin. "If it's wasn't for him then I would—"

"Never have touched a guitar?" Hachi finished my sentence. "I know the whole story, Lu."

I scratched the back of my head, "Yeah...he's all I ever talk about."

"But you sound so different now," I looked at Hachi, trying to understand what they were about to say. "I don't know. From the first time we talked, it sounded like he was some ultimate rockstar who was coincidentally your brother, you know. He's this godly figure who plays rock and other music that isn't rock is considered sacrilege."

I closed my eyes tightly at their description, "Man, I'm sorry."

"Now though? It's like he's your starting point," Hachi placed their focus on me now. They gave a little chuckle. "Don't know if anyone's told you this but, you've got a lot of potential, a fiery one, too."

They looked up again at the starry sky, "Like exploding stars."

There was a sense of nostalgia in that phrase. I could've sworn someone told me that before. They continued, "I see a lot of stars in your eyes and in your friends, too. Even if you'll go your own paths after this camp, you four have something special."

"Thanks," I mumbled, lowering my head, my fingers playing with the grass.

They rubbed Aiden's strap in between their fingers, "where's your guitar?"

"Aiden was nice enough to swap with me," I told them. "I taught him the guitar, and he taught me the uke. Quite easy on my fingers." I wiggled my fingers. Playing the guitar sometimes was a pain, especially with the really complex chords that make my fingers stretch. Hachi hummed.

"Excited to see you perform later."

I perked up, shocked, "You're gonna watch?"

Hachi wrapped their arm around me. It felt like Alex giving me one of her friendly headlocks, "Pshh—do I hate being misgendered? Hell, yeah!" I awkwardly laughed at their way of saying yes. "I gave it some good thought actually. I chatted with Ells, observed you and your friends, and let me tell you, I've never felt this attached to a camper in my five years of being a counselor."

I smiled at their comment. It was worth boasting about. Hell, yeah, losers. Hachi's never felt close to any of you peasants.

Hachi continued, "Yeahhhhh, you guys will kill this! Trust me! The band's name will be written everywhere!"

I smiled, fantasizing our band name everywhere. Then I realized we did not have a band name.

"Our band name!" I screamed. Hachi let me out of their grasp.

With that, I rushed through the woods to the center of the camp site, where counselors and members of the art club were adding final touches to the stage for our performance later.

The stage was a huge wooden platform placed across the main hall. I could see a drum set resting in the middle of the stage. The backdrop was a kaleidoscope of bayanihan butterflies from the Art Club members. Each butterfly had unique handprint wings and they all fluttered around the words "Bayanihan End-Of-Camp Show." Some of the wings were actually made of paper to make them pop out from the backdrop. There were streamers all over the stage and with more butterflies resting on them. The campers who were not participating are starting to crowd the banigs placed in front of the stage.

I ran to the back stage, where all the performers waited. The counselors placed extra banigs on the floor for us to sit on. I spotted Aiden, Dani, and Aerol all sitting comfortably on a red and yellow banig. I collapsed onto the grass and sat cross-legged in front of them.

"You're back, Lu," Aiden smiled. He was practicing the chords on the guitar. Surprisingly, it did not take him a lot of time before he mastered the chords of the song. Hopefully Raymond would see just how much fitted for music Aiden was instead of basketball.

"We're up in a few," Dani was practicing the song on her bass.

"Yo, where did you get the bass?" I pointed to the bass.

"Ellie told Hachi about us performing," Dani glanced at where her fingers were positioned on the fretboard then at her two fingers plucking the thick strings of the bass. "She then gave me this, it's Hachi's."

I was in awe at how nice Ellie was to us.

"Hello, hello, hello, campers of Bayanihan!" Ellie's cheerful voice came through the mic, she was the show host. "We are so excited tonight to see what our performers have prepared for us to commemorate our fun-filled time here!"

"Our band name!" I suddenly remembered. "What's our name?! We need a band name!"

Aerol gave an evil laugh that sounded like a cocky Santa Claus. I had a really bad feeling about this. "Don't worry, Lu," Aerol tossed his drumstick in the air, watched it make a twirl before catching it. "I've got one. A great one."

Nervous and excited, the three of us leaned forward to catch Ellie introducing us.

"Now, introducing our first band! Foes turning friends! Here's the Quadratic Formu-buds!" Ellie stretched our names and roared with all her might as we all glared at Aerol.

"Are you freaking serious?" I asked as we all stood up to walk toward the stairs.

"Why? I think it's genius," Aerol insisted. "Quadra? Four? Us? It's quite well thought of."

"I thought we agreed on Broken Crayons," Dani pouted.

"Broken Crayons sound way, way better than this forced math project," I smirked.

"Hey, Ellie asked me, not you," Aerol defended. I broke into a big smile and rubbed his back. I stopped everyone once we hit the front of the stairs.

"Whatever our name is, let's show everyone what we got. Connect with music, and if you screw up, you're still good looking," I smiled at their sneers before continuing, "Ha on three. One! Two! Three!"

"Ha!" Everyone shouted before jogging energetically up the stage.

Everyone clapped as we walked on stage. The applause was easing as we got our instruments ready. The applause then turned into patient murmurs, campers chatting with their friends to pass time. I twisted the uke around to give it one last tune. The sound of everyone chatting made it difficult for me to separate the chords from the noise. I pursed my lips.

I felt a slight tap on my shoulder and jumped. I felt the strap of Aiden's uke being lifted from my body. Turning around, I caught Ray in a black hoodie. I scanned him and watched his fingers tune Aiden's uke. Aiden did not seem bothered by it. He was too busy reviewing the chords to notice. In case he did, I blocked his view of Raymond even if my small body was not doing much.

"What did you do this time?" I hissed at Raymond, low enough so no one in the audience would hear me. Raymond gave no response and handed back the uke. He gave me a thumbs up as he jumped off the stage and joined his jock friends. My frown remained on my face as I watched him. A few of his friends pushed him with big grins on their faces. Ready to get angry, I began to pluck each string. To my surprise each note sounded right. Guess he can tune shit.

I could not waste any more time. I'll thank him later. Rushing up to the mic, I held it with my free hand.

"Hi!" I was a bit shocked to hear my voice out of the stereo. Everyone applauded. Once it died down, I continued, "Before we start: I'm Lu, Dani on bass, Aerol on drums, and our amazing Aiden on guitar!"

The cheers got Aiden to break out in a huge smile, excitedly waving at everyone. "So, this camp felt like a juvenile at first because my mom just threw me here thinking I could get 'cured' out of whatever phase I was going through." I heard a few campers laugh while others nodded. It made me less tense knowing some kids entered this camp feeling the same way I did. "But! This camp cured me in a way that is totally different from what my mom probably wanted. I reunited with two people after six years, and got to meet some really cool people here: Aiden, Hachi, Ellie, Sayaka and Yukari, to name a few." Shit, am I taking too long?

I scanned the audience. Everyone was sitting down on banigs while the counselors were standing at the back, and I was reminded of the first time I performed in this camp. Kids my age and younger in the front row. Adults at the back.

I remembered Syd's usual line before starting the first song. "Alright, I'll end at that so we have a lifetime to perform for you," I checked to see if everyone was ready to start. The stars in their eyes surrounded me.

"Colony House, You Know it."

Those who knew the song screamed. Aerol banged his stick three times before hitting the high tom on the drum set. Aiden's rapid guitar strumming followed suit. Dani and I soon joined in. We were nearing the first few lines. I glanced around the audience once more in hopes to find someone to focus on.

That was when I spotted two counselors sitting on a bench behind the audience seated in their banigs. A nonbinary producer and a cheerful gal who happily leaned on their shoulder. Those two alone gave me enough serotonin to carry out the whole song.

Stopping my uke, I held onto the mic and closed my eyes before singing the first lines.

Take that picture from your frame.
I'll put it in my pocket so that everyday you're
    with me.
I'll keep it close to my heart.

Dani carried a steady beat with her bass while simultaneously swaying back and forth to add variety to the performance. I turned to her as I sang the next lines, playing my uke and swaying to match with her.

Give me one more kiss before the boys arrive.
Now sugar, San Francisco is a hell of a drive,
But don't worry.
The road is good when the road is long.
And we'll be back before you.

We all stopped moving, smiles on our faces as we sang the chorus:

Knoooooow, you knooooooooow it!

The crowd stood up and joined us in jumping up and down, caught in the energy of the song.

La la la la la la!

I felt like flying. Everyone started to stand up and jump around, singing along to the lyrics and with us. I spotted a counselor holding a camera. Without thinking, I looked directly into it and smiled before carrying on the rest of the song.

Aiden strode to where Dani was playing and the two performed a little back-to-back dance, making the crowd cheer loudly. The two then skipped toward Aerol, who was at the back watching everyone calmly behind his drums. Upon spotting the two, he began laughing. I watched them approach me last with huge grins on their faces. The three of us began to bob our heads crazily as we played our string instruments. Laughing, they returned to their original positions. Aiden stumbled a bit and stared at us with wide eyes as he continued playing. That made us laugh even louder. I caught myself giggling as I sang the song, so I had to snap back immediately to sing properly. The audience was laughing with us too.

I could not help but stare at the night sky, at the moon, and all the tiny, sparkly stars around it. Syd's probably enjoying from the moon. The image of his smile left a sweet taste in my mouth.

The song ended with everyone on their feet, applauding for what seemed like eternity to us. Aerol left his drums to stand in front with us. I checked Aiden and Aerol who stood on my left, then at Dani who was on my right. Holding their hands, we all took a bow before waving goodbye to everyone. Dani led us down the stage while Aiden and Aerol followed behind us.

Sayaka and Yukari were waiting near the stairs, ready for their performance.

21

"What did you prepare?" I asked them, curious.

Sayaka and Yukari looked at each other, lips curving upward before turning to me. "You'll see," says Yukari.

"I'll sit front row then," I was about to turn around to find a spot in the audience area when Sayaka yanked my arm. She brought me close enough for her mouth to reach my ear.

"Meet us at our cabin after," she said in a low voice. I gave her a serious look, nodding.

"Up next are the two trainees from Right Note Philippines! Sayaka and Yukari!" Ellie announced. She waited for them to go up the stairs before retreating from the stage to stay with Hachi. Yukari went up first. She wore a black graphic shirt tee over an oversized long sleeved red and black striped shirt, tucked into a pair of black ripped jeans. She topped it off with a pair of Doc Martens. She stood, hands politely resting on her stomach as her head was lowered, waiting for the song to start. The crowd anticipated in silence. There were a few whispers here and there, which seemed to distract Yukari. She placed a hand on her chest to calm her down.

"Sorry, may I sit here?" I whispered to two campers in the front row. Silently, they parted to make space for me. I thanked them quietly before squeezing in between them.

There was still adrenaline pumping in my veins from the performance earlier, and without any hesitation, I shouted, "You got this Yukari!"

Yukari did not lift her head, but I could see her cheeks rise as she smiled. Right after, a Korean pop song started playing. I recognized the song immediately since I heard Sachiko played it once during our practices. It was an energetic track full of jumping and trendy dance moves. Yukari chose to start the song from the pre-chorus to build up the tension for the chorus.

She lip-synced to a deep, raspy yet excited female voice, "You ready? Let's go!" She stuck out her tongue in a smile, ready to hit the dance break as the music played loudly. Her smile never left her face. The upbeat song faded out as Yukari finished the chorus. It's wild to think she's only been doing this for a few months. Yukari knelt down as the song transitioned into a rather bad-ass sounding beat. She then left the centerstage to give the spotlight to her partner.

Sayaka rushed into position on stage. Her expression went from frightened to fierce to match the song. She wore a cropped tee exposing her midriff and paired it with a pair of black high waisted shorts. Her lips were painted dark red, adding an extra ounce of fierceness to her attire. The whole look managed to show off her personality while still having the same color scheme as Yukari's.

Sayaka began to catwalk toward the front of the stage as the song transitioned to the pre-chorus. A different female voice sang powerfully as Sayaka showcased her flexibility and accuracy as she moved her legs smoothly, hitting every beat. The chorus came and she smirked as she lip-synced the lines.

Once the beat dropped, so did she. She pulled out a side lunge and the whole crowd went wild. She did it with such ease. There was really something mesmerizing about Sayaka. She was formidable at dancing. The music was following her more than the opposite. She owned the music. This was what four to five years of hardcore practice could result in. Damn.

She pulled herself up, her feet began to move rapidly as she spun around to the beat, stopping and posing at the last syllable. The same line played a second time, and this time, Yukari joined her onstage and the two spun around to the mesmerizing words.

At the end of the line, the music faded out and the two girls were already positioned for their last song. Sayaka knelt on the ground, facing the side of the stage while Yukari stood in front, her head lowered as she waited for the music. Everyone applauded Sayaka and Yukari's solos, but the cheers became louder when campers realized they would both dance together.

Synthesized music filled the air, but my mind perceived fantasy. I saw Yukari and Sayaka turning to the audience as they began to move in harmony, complementing one another's different styles. Yukari's smile glowed as she faced Sayaka's sassy grin. They definitely improved from the last time I saw them in that garden full of unique flowers and fluttering butterflies. I saw them smiling, conversing, and giggling with each other.

When the flowers of various colors bloom
And the flower petals flutter off

From behind the stage, I saw Dani rush toward me.

"What's wrong?"

"Let's join them!" Dani cut me off. She grabbed my wrist and pulled me up the stairs. I saw Sayaka lip-syncing.

Just remember this one thing

Yukari spotted us and her smile grew wider. She rushed to pull us to the center before her line, and winked.

It's now

I did not have time for regret, even if it embraced me from behind. I watched Sayaka and tried to recall the dance moves. I caught myself laughing at how stupid I looked. From the corner of my eye, I caught Dani smiling, too. Our eyes met and our smiles could not leave our faces. They just grew bigger and bigger.

It's my fiesta!

Dani and I froze as we watched Sayaka and Yukari move individually but totally complementing each other. I looked at Dani who shrugged. I watched her attempt to do a weird step, copying Yukari and Sayaka. She failed and giggled. I tried it myself, and once I lifted my leg, I placed it down immediately. I heard Dani laugh at me. Then Sayaka and Yukari turned around and held our hands. Dani and I just went with the flow, the four of us jumped around in a circle as the song continued.

"Pose in three, two, now!" Sayaka instructed.

The four of us strutted our own poses. Sayaka and Yukari mastered their individual poses while Dani and I settled awkwardly. I forced a smile, already cursing myself at the pose my brain automatically instructed my body. There were a gazillion better poses to make and I just had to pull out a peace sign. I did slightly better than Dani though. She just stood there sideways and glared at a far distance.

I broke out in laughter as Dani began breathing heavily as if she was the one who performed all three songs. Sayaka and Yukari turned to see why I was laughing and broke character immediately. Yukari knelt on the stage laughing so hard while Sayaka was covering her mouth trying to hold in her laughter. Dani relished the moment, seeing all three of us having a fit. Then we held each other's hands and bowed together to the nonstop applause.

Ellie went on stage, "Thank you so much, Sayaka and Yukari. Thank you, Lu and Dani! Sayaka and Yukari, we'll await your debut soon!"

Sayaka and Yukari bowed once more as Dani and I hurried down the stage.

22

"You may come in," Sayaka slightly opened the door to their cabin. It looked exactly like mine and Dani's. There were two beds facing each other with two nightstands and suitcases on the floor, opened and filled with clothes and toiletries.

"Yukari's in the shower. Sorry."

"No prob," I said.

Sayaka straightened out the plain blue blanket on her bed, patting a spot for me to sit on. I removed my Birks and sat where she asked me to sit. I turned to see a little octopus plushie on her bed.

"What's its name, Sayaka?" I asked, petting the plushie.

"Puka," Sayaka replied softly. I widened my eyes.

"Wait, what—"

"Pu-ka," Sayaka placed an emphasis on the 'k' sound. "It's a floating sound in Japanese."

I felt a gush of relief travel through my body. "Oh," I awkwardly laughed. Sayaka did not seem to get my joke. She stared at me without a word. Her facial expression was as stiff as a rock. I began to blink really quickly, wondering if I had to apologize for mishearing her. She narrowed her eyes before widening them. She bent down and rummaged through her ecobag, the one she used when she was practicing in the forest. She threw a pack of Oreos onto my lap.

And not just any kind of Oreo. Golden Oreos.

My mouth dropped, words not coming out of my mouth. Sayaka did not let me say anything else. She placed a finger on her lips.

"We got them from the mess hall, sshhh," Yukari stepped out of the bathroom, a towel wrapped around her shoulders to catch the water droplets from her long hair. She placed her finger on her lips as well, then smiled.

I noticed how different their pajamas were. Sayaka liked wearing cute matching pajamas of crescent moons and shooting stars while Yukari enjoyed wearing biker shorts and baseball tees to sleep.

When Yukari reached Sayaka, she nudged her.

"Give it to her, Saya," Yukari whispered in Japanese. Sayaka rolled her eyes at her, rummaged once more through her ecobag, and handed me a lavender envelope with a cute bunny sticker. It said, "To Lu" plus a character written in hiragana.

"That says ru," Yukari pointed to the character. "Sayaka wrote it." I turned to Sayaka, who looked embarrassed.

"Just open it," as she looked away from the envelope. Carefully, I unsealed the envelope and found eight tickets inside.

"Right Note Rookie Showcase, Olympic Hall, Seoul, South Korea!" I screamed in delight.

"You told us that you were in a band, right?" Yukari explained, pointing to the tickets. "Five members?"

My heart sank at the thought of Maxxed Out, "Oh, um, yeah. I didn't think you'd remember."

"Then the other three are for Dani, Aiden, and Aerol," Sayaka added.

I looked at the three extra tickets and smiled in realization. The three of us exchanged smiles before falling silent once again.

"To be honest," Yukari sat on the edge of the bed. "We didn't know what to do with the tickets." I looked straight into her eyes, nodding at every word, and not minding Yukari avoiding my eyes as she stared at her feet touching the cold cabin floor. "We actually wanted to throw them into the river. We were sent to this camp because Sayaka and I weren't on good terms."

Sayaka nodded, "Our manager told all the trainees that whoever can prove themselves worthy of debuting would get to perform at the Right Note Rookie Show to represent Right Note Philippines."

I took a closer look at the ticket. 'The trainees of Right Note Philippines (RNPH)' popped out, no further details after that.

"Our CEO told us that if we keep on fighting, no one debuts," Sayaka sat on the other edge of the bed. She played with her fingers. "You told us you were in a band, with Sachiko. I was mad because you had teammates."

"We actually thought that Dani was a part of your band until we learned you two were not on good terms either, like us," Yukari placed her hands on her thighs and played with her fingers. They were looking at different directions, the atmosphere was silent, tensed, and sad.

"We were going to throw the tickets," Sayaka gulped. She stopped playing with her fingers. "But we saw Dani jump into the river."

My breathing paused. They saw it!

"We hid in the trees so you wouldn't see us," Yukari turned to face me, but her eyes focused somewhere on the floor. Her voice was shaky.

She took a deep breath, "We watched from afar how you just dived in to save her, even if you said you hated water." She lifted her eyes to look directly at me. Her pupils were a beautiful shade of dark brown.

"You really showed us that even if you hate the other person so much, you can still change," I froze when she began blinking and tears gracefully plopped onto the blanket, staining it.

"We were inspired," Sayaka did not want to face me. "We wanted to change, too. We wanted to debut. Together." Her lips barely moved.

Yukari lightly wiped the tears from the corner of her eyes, "That was our first time since training period that we practiced happily." She swallowed her saliva and smiled at me. "You really helped us improve ourselves, Lu."

"I really enjoy dancing," Sayaka turned to me at last. "I want to be on stage so damn bad. So damn bad that I shut out everyone and only wanted to focus on debuting. Being sent to this camp, I learned that, I don't want to debut without Yukari." The two looked at each other and tried not to laugh. Something definitely changed in the way they saw each other.

They stood up from their beds and faced me, tear stains on their cheeks, and smiles on their lips that were brighter than the moon.

"In Japan, we bow to show thankfulness and respect," Yukari wiped her eyes. "I'm sure you already knew that already." Yukari and Sayaka slowly bent at 90 degrees angle. I knelt on the bed, crawling my way toward them.

"No-no-no-no— It's totally fine! No need to bow!" I freaked out.

I did not deserve this much respect, especially coming from these two ace performers. I was just a girl with a short temper who played guitar. "It's totally fine!" I scratched my nape. "Stop, please."

Yukari and Sayaka stood up, wiping their eyes while smiling. Immediately, I jumped out of bed and rushed to the girls, embracing them in a tight hug. I rested my head on their shoulders as they squeezed back.

Then we heard a creak. We turned sideways to face the door immediately. Aerol's head popped out.

"I was wondering where you guys went," he sounded worried.

"Ah, don't worry," I rubbed Sayaka and Yukari's back one last time before walking to Aerol.

"Uy, let us enter too," Dani squeaked behind Aerol.

"Mooooove!" Aiden roared.

We laughed as Aerol opened the door wide to let Dani and Aiden in. Aiden dusted his shoulders and punched Aerol, "You followed them here?"

Aerol rolled his eyes while the rest of us laughed at the sight of everyone in one small space. Dani took a deep breath after laughing and turned to the bed.

"Oreos!" Dani's eyes widened. She went straight for the box of golden Oreos I left on the bed.

"Share with us naman, Dan," I whined. She picked up the box and hugged it tightly, giving me a pout before melting into a smile and approaching us with the Oreos.

I crossed my legs as I sat down on the floor, eyes monitoring the pack of Oreos like a CCTV. Dani sat next to me and placed the Oreos in front of us and proceeded to open it immediately. Sayaka sat next to me while Yukari sat next to Dani. Aiden and Aerol followed, sitting between the two trainees.

"Feel free to get some!" Yukari pulled her ecobag and poured on the floor a bunch of chips she must have brought from Japan or 7-11.

"How did you manage to get these?" Sayaka picked up a cylindrical snack with a cat winking on the wrapper. Yukari placed a finger on her lips and winked. Sayaka smiled in response and opened the snack. I watched Sayaka eat the chips, her eyes grew big, she seemed swept away by a pang of nostalgia, and pure thankfulness for Yukari.

Aiden and Aerol took hold of the conversation, talking about Aerol's experiences working at a fastfood chain and Aiden's obsession with Breaking Daylights. Sayaka and Yukari, who were just as clueless as I was with the band, leaned forward as they absorbed everything that came out of Aiden's mouth.

Dani and I did not bother touching any of the other snacks. We had our Oreos and that was all we needed. I focused on my strange way of eating Oreos. Alex called it one of my quirks just so it could pass off as a compliment. I did not eat the whole thing nor did I twist, lick, and dunk it. I simply just separated the cookie and the cream. I kept the cream, and handed the cookie over to—

I looked down and noticed a perfect slice of cream on Dani's palm. Her fingertips touched the edge of the cookie I unconsciously passed to her. We blinked at each other before laughing awkwardly.

"Got used to it," Dani gently placed the cream on my palm.

"Man, Alex would give me the weirdest face when I would pass her my cookies," I handed her my cookie in return. Dani widened her eyes and nodded furiously too.

"Carla too! She goes 'What am I going to do with it?'"

"Oh, sweet! Tickets!" Aiden grabbed the lavender envelope. "For whose concert?"

"For our concert," Yukari shyly raised her hand. "Our showcase."

"If we make it," Sayaka nudged her.

"Oh, yeah. You guys are K-Pop idols, right?" Aiden excitedly asked. Sayaka covered her mouth and scoffed, while Yukari felt her cheeks grew red.

"No! No!" Yukari giggled while objecting, waving her hands left and right. "But, if we do good, then maybe." Her voice rose as she imagined herself debuting with Sayaka.

"We want to show you all that we can do better," Sayaka held Yukari's hand and held it proudly up in the air. "We will show you a good stage together." It was refreshing to see the kids evolve from enemies to teammates.

We chatted for a few more minutes until Aerol decided it was time for us to return to our own cabins.

"We have to pack our stuff," he reasoned, looking at his watch. "Hope no one forgets anything!"

"Lu and I will get going too," Dani joined.

"Don't forget us when you go big," Aerol placed his large hand on Sayaka's shoulder, showcasing his dad-smile. Sayaka gave him a bro hug.

"Ikaw talaga," I muttered. Dani gave an empty laugh as we watched the two.

Sayaka showed us her fist as she slowly placed it on her heart. Like claws coming out of wolverine's hands, her pointer, middle, and thumb spiked up and stayed on her chest. In a low voice, she said, "I won't forget you."

Yukari broke into laughter, shaking Sayaka excitedly.

"Sayaka! Sayaka!" Aiden called her attention before imitating her sign. "I won't forget you either."

"We won't forget you either," Sayaka and Yukari chorused in response.

"Oh, um…may I hug you?" Aiden asked. Sayaka looked a bit shocked to be asked that, but looked happy after a bit of processing.

She opened her arms wide, "Of course!"

Aiden proceeded to hug Sayaka. Then Yukari joined. Then Dani. I came forward. Then Aerol enveloped all of us in his embrace.

♪♪

I waited for everyone to leave Sayaka and Yukari's cabin before asking them for one more thing.

"Could I have one more ticket?" I asked them in a hushed tone.

"Sure!" Yukari rushed to her luggage to look for an extra ticket.

"Why?" Sayaka asked earnestly.

"For my mom," I answered confidently.

23

"Packing's a pain in the ass," Dani plopped on her bed that was still messy with unfolded camp shirts and wrinkled pajamas. We were only 10 minutes into packing and had not even started gathering our supplies from the bathroom.

"It's because you scattered all your things everywhere," I rolled my shirt up and squeezed it into the corner of my luggage. Dani could only groan. I rolled two more shirts and inserted around the insides of my luggage. "Let's sleep together outside."

"I'm sorry, what—"

"You heard me," I turned to see Dani's confused face.

Dani's head fell back on her bed, "But it's so windy outside."

"I slept outside one night and it was perfectly fine," I reminded her. "I'm sure you can handle it. Besides, it's not like we're going to use a shoe and a wet towel as a pillow and blanket."

Dani sat up, her lips formed a straight line as she stared at the wall. She licked her lips, "Fine."

♪♪

We gazed at the same starry sky, only this time without the stress of our performance. Slowly, we laid down on the grass, holding in our screams as tips of the grass tickled our exposed skin.

Dani broke the silence, "When was the last time we slept like this?"

"Seven years ago."

"You do know the stars we see now are the same stars that people saw millions of years ago?"

"Mm," I hummed.

"You ever wondered if those people who saw these stars ever marvelled at them?"

"Don't most people think that?"

"I think the stars look wonderful," Dani used her hands as a pillow. "How brilliant they are, but most people seem to overlook their brilliance and just see them as small dots in the sky."

"Like your freckles."

Dani sat up, "My freckles?"

"Yeah," I remained on the ground. "They are pretty visible in the daytime."

Dani paused for a bit, "I thought no one would notice. They're just small—"

"Small dots on your face to others," I finished her sentence. "But I think they look wonderful on you."

We stayed silent for a bit.

"I don't like my freckles," Dani opened up. "I know there are people out there who wished they had freckles instead of acne, but...I want acne more than freckles...because I don't really like my freckles...or my face, or this body, or this li—"

Faith, trust, and pixie dust
I've got it all up my sleeve
Captain Hook's slurs won't work on me
We'll fly up, up just grab my hand

Dani listened as I sang the lines and she continued the rest.

We'll fly off to neverland

"Just because I sing about these things doesn't mean I act like it," she insisted. "I'm ugly as hell, Lu." Dani gave a soft sigh, relieved that she finally told someone.

"And that's what makes you beautiful."

"The fudge."

"You're really messy for someone who seems so organized in their dumb private school uniform. You made me sleep outside; I got a fever because of you. You didn't even try to invite me to the swimming pool with your friends."

"Wow, thanks a lot—"

"But you were so quick to make friends because of your extroverted nature," I kept my eyes on the stars. "It must be hard to put up a front as a pastel girl when your life is just monochromatic. Your eyes become the moon, making the constellations on your eyes shine beautifully when you smile."

"Lu, shut up," Dani mumbled.

"To act all tough and positive in front of everyone at such a young age is damn cool. Your laugh makes the angels fly around heaven in utter joy, while your wrinkled face when you cry and tears fall down your cheeks freaking hurts me."

"Lu?"

"I wish I could wipe the tears off your small face when we fight, just lightly, gently. Sorry, Dani. For being an ass."

It was warm for a few seconds. It seemed I had all the stars from the black sky in my palms, all warm and illuminating. They created this heat, like a longing that was finally satisfied. It was as if the other stars that couldn't fit in my hands entered my body, lighting up every corner, every nook inside me. They danced around, twirled ever so happily in my chest. I heard rustling right after, which I'm guessing was from Dani. Silence.

"I'm so—" Dani tried to say.

"I—" I cut her.

Silence again.

"No, I—"

"It's oka—"

We kept on talking over each other. I started to crack up.

"What's so funny, Lu?" Dani hit my chest with the back of her hand. "Uy, tell me."

I took deep breaths, held her hand. and traced a heart on her palm. It was an imperfect and rather small one. She giggled.

"I'm sorry, Dani." She nodded.

We held hands for a bit, finding comfort in each other's presence.

"I'm sleepy," Dani blurted.

"Then sleep."

"You sleep," Dani scoffed. "You've been talking a lot lately."

I ignored her and closed my eyes, as my fingers continued to trace hearts on her palm. I memorized the lines on her palms like the chords in a song, the texture like lyrics, and the size of her palm compared to mine like a beat.

"Be honest with me," Dani started again. "You have a fear of the water." It was a declaration.

"Yes, I never told you about it, I guess." I kept my eyes closed. "A huge one."

She sat up. "I only guessed by the way you acted when we were swimming."

Recalling that memory, I took a deep breath.

"Yet you jumped in the water," Dani recounted. "Why, Lu?"

I chuckled at my response, "Sex, drugs, rock 'n' roll, Dan."

"Syd said that a lot, I remember," Dani laid down again. "What does that mean anyway?"

"Something you say when you're about to do something stupid."

"But, what does that really mean?"

"Good question," I stopped for a bit. "We do shit that are deemed stupid by society but we do them anyway out of defiance or just for pleasure. Probably why Kuya would say it before doing something dumb. Like when he jumped off the roof of my aunt's house along with my cousins and onto the backyard swimming pool."

"Why would he do that?"

"Sex, drugs, rock 'n' roll."

Dani took a deep breath. "I see it as something that can connect people," she said.

I thought a bit more about her interpretation, "To connect people, hmmm. You know, that makes a lot of sense."

"What's your take?"

"You know how rock 'n' roll is seen as demonic music? Sex and drugs din."

"Yeah, but that's debatable."

"It's just what society wants us to believe. By saying sex, drugs, rock 'n' roll, we're claiming ourselves as free people. Screw society. We're our own people. That's how we're connected, by being diverse."

I remember what Ellie said. The beauty of humanity, so diverse yet so connected.

Dani hummed in agreement, then gave a soft exhale. "It's a broad concept," she said.

"Probably."

"We could end at how rebelling against the repressive norms makes us feel free.'"

"Probably," I nodded.

"I think that's a nice way to end it for now."

"I think so, too."

We were both getting sleepy, the wind became our lullaby, and our eyes were struggling to stay open.

"Don't leave me the way Syd did," I whispered before drifting off to sleep. "That's all I ask."

I heard Dani give a breathless laugh before whispering back, "I promise."

24

The mess hall was crowded with parents and campers. The counselors prepared huge 'Till We Meet Again!' cards on different colored cartolinas and stuck them on the walls. I sat outside with my camp friends to avoid the noisy crowd inside.

I watched girls cry in each other's arms and boys promising to play together online. Some campers ran to their parents with their new friend, while others stopped by to chat with Ellie. The kids were quite happy seeing their parents, wrapping their arms around them, and blabbering nonstop about their stay here.

My eyes darted from parent to parent, looking for my mom, and on the verge of crying because she was nowhere. I shook my head and decided to focus on who were with me right now. That was when I spotted a few campers with their phones as they surrounded four girls and a tall man who was trying to make way for them.

"Move!"

Ellie caught the commotion and asked the crowd to wait for their parents inside the mess hall. As the crowd thinned, the group came toward us. The girls were dressed casually but they looked like Korean idols hiding their faces from the paparazzi. Two wore bucket hats with masks on while the other two wore shades.

From the corner of my eye, I saw Yukari and Sayaka rushed up to them. Both were drowned in hugs, and there were giggles and screams. One of the bucket hat girls took off her mask and smiled at us, showing her dimples.

"Yu! Saya! How was hell with each other?" She ruffled Sayaka's hair as she asked them in Korean.

Yukari released herself from the group hug and turned to us. Politely, she introduced us to her guests. "Lu, Aiden, Aerol, Dani," Yukari named each one of us.

Then she introduced her guests, "Guys, meet our members! Yna, Yujin, Hyunjin, Soyeon."

"Holy shit! I can't believe I'm actually meeting a real girl group," Aiden's mouth dropped. Sayaka playfully slapped him, which drew oooohs from the members.

The girl who ruffled Sayaka's hair asked, "Are they your friends?"

"Yes, Yna," Sayaka said.

"Are you guys going to our showcase?" Soyeon asked. She had bright blue locks that reminded me of Gatorade.

"Soyeon! Ask them if Sayaka and Yukari have been good," suggested Yujin, her blond hair showing under her black bucket hat. Yukari and Sayaka were shaking their heads in response, but Soyeon ignored them and walked up to us, removing her glasses.

"Were they good?" I saw her dark brown eyes up close, big and glowing as if they've been neatly polished. I could stare at her eyes all day.

I snapped myself out of my fascination and turned to the rest of the Quadratic Formu-buds for the answer. Dani waved her hand at me, Aerol and Aiden nodded at her. It was up to me to respond but I could not find the words.

"Not good girl!" Yujin shouted behind Soyeon, causing everyone to laugh uncontrollably while Sayaka and Yukari shook her shoulders.

Seeing them both acting childlike toward Yna, Yujin, Hyunjin, and Soyeon made me less nervous. I turned back to Soyeon, who was still waiting for my answer.

I replied confidently, "No." Sayaka and Yukari looked betrayed. Soyeon was squinted her eyes at me. I added, "They were the best!" I emphasized the last word with raised arms.

Applause greeted my confirmation, but Yna chose to tease Yukari and Sayaka. "Ayeeeeee, she's lying!"

"Hey! She said they were the best! They were the best!" Soyeon's imitation was both charming and funny that everyone laughed.

"Saya, who's that boy over there?" Hyunjin, the tallest member with a beauty mark under her eye and short black hair, pointed at Aiden.

"Aiden," Sayaka motioned Aiden to join her. "This is my friend Hyunjin."

"Annyeonghaseyo, Hyunjin-ssi," Aiden placed his hands on his stomach and bowed. When he straightened up, he looked at Sayaka and Hyunjin who were both amazed at him. A blushing Hyunjin bowed back.

"You can speak Korean?" Hyunjin asked. Her husky voice cracked at the last syllable. Aerol, Dani and I suppressed our laughs seeing Aiden freeze at Hyunjin's question.

Sayaka squeezed his shoulder, "Good job, Aiden!" She also gave him a thumbs up. Aiden smiled back at her, confident at delivering his greeting.

Yna came forward and addressed us, "Thank you so much for taking care of our Sayaka and Yukari!" She forced Sayaka and Yukari to bow with her. The four of us bowed back in response.

Just then, the tall man whispered something into Yukari's ear with a stern look. Her smile faded away as she pouted, "We have to leave now."

"Bye, everyone," Sayaka waved sadly, preparing to leave.

I was about to wave back at her, but then I decided to do something more memorable. I showed her a fist, drew it close to my chest, as my my pointer, pinky, and thumb shot out. I mouthed, "Bye, Sayaka."

Sayaka's smile could not get any bigger. She grabbed my wrist and embraced me tightly. She rested her head on my shoulder as her hand caressed the back of my head. She let go after three seconds with a slightly calmer smile.

"Wait!" Dani pulled up her star-themed phone and bellowed, "Group photo!"

I casually wrapped my arm around Dani, placing my head close to hers and looking up at the camera. Our band and Sayaka's group crowded behind us, trying their best to get in the shot. We gave our best smiles then bade each other goodbye.

"See you at the showcase!" Yukari shouted.

"Ganbare!" I shouted back.

♪♪

Dani saw something from afar and squinted to confirm that what she was seeing was whoever it was. "Crap, my mom is here. If she sees me with you, we're dead."

I laughed at her exaggeration, "Who are we? Romeo and Juliet?"

Dani rummaged through the front pocket of her backpack and brought out a pentel pen. Quickly, she drew an imperfect heart on my palm. She showed me an imperfect heart on her palm as she waved goodbye, "Probably."

I laughed, totally amused. I stared at the drawing, feeling like the luckiest kid on this planet. I turned to see Aiden and Aerol staring at me, smiling from ear to ear.

"Damn to whatever you two are thinking," I gnashed my teeth but pretended to smile. Aerol and Aiden stiffened.

"Oh! My mom's here! I'll skedaddle now." Aerol slung his huge camouflage backpack over his shoulder, "Aiden, you have my phone number, right?"

"Yep! Saved it on my phone. The World's Gr8est Drummer!" Aiden proudly showed his phone with Aerol's number on it. Aerol gave his fatherly smile, bro-hugging Aiden, and giving me a tight embrace before walking toward his mom.

"Aiden! There's my man!" A tall dark-skinned man placed his hands on Aiden's shoulder. If Aiden was already a tower next to me, his dad was a freaking skyscraper. Their smiles were identical. Aiden took a lot after his dad.

"You must be Lu," Aiden's dad looked at me. His voice sounded like a narrator of a nature documentary. I nodded as I shook his hand. "Thank you for standing up for my boy," he said.

Before letting my hand go, he added, "Thank you for existing."

I was caught off guard. With a smile, I told him, "Your son is an excellent guitarist. Make him play more, please. He's got potential, a bright one."

Aiden's face lit up at my words, "May our paths cross again." He adjusted his backpack as he stepped backward to follow his dad.

I nodded right back at him, "May they cross."

I watched their backs grow smaller and smaller as Aiden began to talk about the Formu-buds and meeting a girl group, his dad listening attentively at his every word. An empty void swelled within me. It would have been pretty cool to have a father. I should have been used to this feeling by now, but here I was, pretty jealous of Aiden having a father.

Too caught up in their dynamic, I felt a light tap on my shoulder. Hoping it was my mom, I turned around quickly, only to find it was Raymond. My smile immediately dropped, surprising him.

"What?" My voice went a whole 180.

"Chill, man." He handed me a bunch of beautifully woven bracelets. One was a zigzag of green, white, and black. Another was a duet of yellow and dark blue. There were also dark red, black, and blue. "My mom makes these. Give them to whoever you like."

"You aren't giving them to your basketball friends?"

"They didn't teach me anything significant."

I took all the bracelets and thanked him, "They're really beautiful."

Silently, two women approached us. One with skin as pale as a daisy's petal, and the other with skin as brown and gorgeous as the smooth wood of an oak. "Come on, Ray," the brown-skinned woman ruffled Raymond's hair. The pale skinned woman smiled at me. Her freckles looked so much like Dani's. Raymond did not say anything, only mouthing me a 'thank you' before walking away holding both their hands. I did not know how to respond.

I was still processing the scene when I heard Mom's voice, I did not expect the rush of serotonin flowing out of my body at the sound of my name on her lips. I turned around and took in her fancy monochromatic suit and a silk blouse with bright, pink roses. Her presence drowned out the crowd of kids crying and sniffing, of parents chatting with their kids, and of counselors discussing in groups.

"Let's go?" I missed her voice so much.

I held back tears of joy as I responded, "Yeah, I'm hungry."

25

For the first time, Mom let me sit in front while she drove our trusted Vios. I cradled my phone and earphones, just in case the silence would be long enough for me to listen to a few tunes. I was hoping though that we could start a conversation. Minutes passed, I stared at my phone's black screen, and the small heart Dani drew on my hand was peeking out from behind the device.

"I saw you playing," My mom's voice sent chills down my spine. A black hole of questions and worries began to grow and eat up my organs.

Shitshitshit.

"You want to explore Syd's room?"

I turned to her. Her eyes did not move away from the road nor did her mouth curl upward. She was serious about opening Syd's room. "Yeah," I relaxed and leaned back on my seat. "Yeah."

♪♪

Mom opened the main door that led to the second floor of the house. I always entered with my head down so I would not see Syd's door. I stood next to my mom, my heart racing as she held onto the slightly rusted doorknob to insert a rarely used key. I heard the click and held in my breath.

Nothing changed. Syd's Kurt Cobain poster was still on the ceiling, next to a poster of a monkey holding a banana like a gun. His wooden desk on the left part of the wall was filled with papers and textbooks. His blanket was crumpled and nearly falling off his bed in the center of the room. His guitar rested peacefully on top of it. The room smelt of cedar wood, it was his favorite perfume.

"Lu, sit here." Mom sat down on the floor, facing Syd's messy closet and his bathroom door that was partially open. There were pieces of clothing thrown on the floor, next to her was a plain white undershirt meant for school that Syd liked wearing to sleep.

I crossed my legs as I slowly lowered myself onto the wooden floor. Both of us were facing the same way as I did not want to look at Mom. I did not think there was anything that deserved a dressing-down nor commendation.

My brain was telling me to talk to her, to ask her how she heard about my performance. Did she like it? Would she be okay with Maxxed Out and the Battle of the Bands?

Someone was inside my head. Messing with my brain. It went, "Ask her! Ask her, Lu! Come on. Don't chicken out. You aren't a chicken, right? Unless you are. Oh, dear. Are you a freaking chicken? What are you going to do? Flap your little chicken wings? Huh? You wimp. Ask her! Just! Ask! Her! Now! Go!

"Mom—" I had to stop the other voice from talking too much and humiliating me.

"Yes, Lu?" Mom seemed happy that I asked.

"How did you f-find out 'bout the c-camp thing?" I stammered.

"Oh. Tita Rochelle told me the camp held live streams for their end parties," Mom replied.

Once she mentioned it, the memory of a familiar face filming us appeared vividly in my head. I widened my eyes at the thought that I was performing live that night. And that mom must've seen me perform with the Formu-buds and Sayaka and Yukari.

I'm damned. I did not say a word, just stared at Mom's knees, guessing that she must have tucked her feet under her butt. She only sat like that when she needed to have a very serious conversation with me. On most times, she would tell me about how colleges would want my resumes to be filled with activities aside from musical events. It was her way of trying to get me out of this path. That pretty much explained why I stopped getting nervous around her whenever she sat like that. Eight out of nine times, it would be a one-way talk about music.

"Dani was there pala," Mom tried to continue the conversation. "How is she?"

"She's good," I spoke in a louder voice. Nodding to her so she could continue with what she was going to say next. "Good," I repeated.

"How about Maya, Alex, Sachiko, and Emmie?"

I winced upon hearing their names. "I knew you'd bring this up," I scratched my eyes then pinched the bridge of my nose.

Mom scooted closer, putting her smooth hands on mine. She caressed the back of my hands with her thumb. "Lu, that night you arrived home from the clubhouse, you barely said a word and just went to sleep. I thought something happened to yo—"

I forced a crooked smile as my voice shook at my last sentence. "We're good." Out of all the lies I told her, this one hurt me the most. I recalled Alex saying they weren't even near the word 'almost.' Plus the dumbass. I kept my eyes on Mom's hands that covered mine with patience. She stopped caressing them, but did not let go.

"Lu, what happened?" She was peeking at my face, trying to make contact with my eyes.

"I— I don't know." I was annoyed at her question. Tears fell anyway as words stumbled out of my mouth.

"I just— Kuya made this band and— and Dani and Aerol left— I got mad at them— and then I got mad at Maya for screwing up while we were practicing and then everyone— and then everyone got pissed at me and left. They all left me, Mom!"

I took deep breaths, gasping as memories rushed in. Mom did not say anything, but she waited patiently. She hummed to tell me that she was listening.

"I'm just—trying to keep Kuya's band. It's the only thing I have left of Kuya, Mom."

Soft gasps became bellows for air as emotions that simmered rose to the top of my throat. I wept as I held on to Mom's hands, tightly as my tears spilled out.

"Mom, I feel like I'm losing everyone."

I wailed and gripped her hand for dear life, but she did not wriggle out of my hold nor unclasped my hands. She allowed me to squeeze her hands and let me scream out my bottled emotions. She never let me go.

"Kuya shouldn't have died, Mom," I screamed from desperation. "It should have been m—"

"Never say that, Lu. Never!"

She unclasped my hold on her hands, closed the space between us, and cupped my face, I stopped screaming and sobbing. I gasped for air as I waited for her to talk.

"You are a blessing in this cursed world," she smiled while searching my eyes for answers. "Lu, without you, I would be very, very sad, and alone." Mom said those words slowly, tears welling in her eyes. But I responded with a breathless laugh. i tried hard not to picture my mom weeping alone for the loss of her two children.

"All I have now is you, Lu. Don't let go of us." Mom pleaded, wiping the tears off my face. I was seeing her in a new light. She was also heartbroken but she was holding it together for the two of us. How petty of me to think that she was not grieving for her son in the same way that I was grieving for my brother.

Her revelation shocked me though. "I made a very similar mistake with my band years ago."

"You were in a band?!" I almost shrieked at her. Disbelief was written all over my face.

"Do I not look like I was in one?"

"You look like you could be in a church choir, not in a band."

She calmly laughed as she pushed my hair behind my ear, "Thank you, anak." She then pointed to Syd's guitar resting on his bed, "Now, that guitar. Why do you think it looks so worn out?"

Hmmm. Tough question. "Because… Kuya played with it a lot?"

Mom flicked my forehead. "It's because it was mine before it was his."

Oh.

She stood up and grabbed the guitar from the bed. Then she returned to our spot and positioned the guitar on her thigh before proceeding to pluck each string to make sure the guitar was in tune before playing.

"Ay, naku. Your brother always came down late for lunch because of his guitar, but he can't even tune the strings properly? Ano ba yan?"

I snickered at Mom's comment. She smiled after hearing a perfectly tuned guitar, gracefully plucking a familiar melody to express her happiness. There was something about that melody that brought butterflies in my stomach.

"Kuya played this before," I finally realized.

Mom finished the melody with a smile that could turn winter into spring, "I missed playing this song."

I squished the bottom of my lip, thinking hard of the name of the song, "I could've sworn I've heard Aiden play this at camp. He said it was from some band called Breg something."

"Breaking Daylights, anak," Mom corrected me, a bit annoyed. I saw that when she raised her eyebrow.

I shrugged, "Must've been an old band."

Mom looked at me, "Anak, it was my band."

"Oh," I blankly responded. Mom smiled.

"Ohhh!" Then I connected the dots.

"Oohhhhh!"

"Yes, anak."

Syd knew and never told me. He was right about Mom and me. Mom's smile at my delayed realization was priceless. I just did not know.

"So, what happened to you, guys?" I quickly added, "Aiden said you were ahead of your time." Mom let out a loud laugh this time, leaning back and arching her head.

"Let me meet this Aiden kid someday!" Her eyes went serious as she prepared to tell me her story, "Anak, I had this group of friends whom I thought would stay with me past grad school. Although, when Cheryl passed away… I was so caught up in what happened that—"

A soft laugh escaped her. She still had the guitar in her hands. Scanning it, she pursed her lips.

"That was the last song we performed before disbanding," a shaky sigh escaped her lips. "It was a song we loved so much. The girls loved seeing Syd and listening to him singing our songs, playing our music. Cheryl was the one who was always excited to see Syd. She was the one who…"

Mom paused to wipe a tear. "Cheryl taught Syd that song."

She looked up to hold back her from tears, but she continued. "They never saw him master the song as if it was his own."

Seeing mom and hearing her story really broke me. Mom loved Tita Cheryl intensely, like a sister. I could not imagine how she could have moved on.

"I had an outburst just like you," Mom continued. I sensed pure regret. "I shouted things I regretted saying. And just like that, the only people I called my friends walked out of the studio door."

This hit me real hard because this happened to me. Mom's story was similar to mine it was pretty scary. I did not want to lose my friends just because I was stuck in the past.

"Have you ever contacted your bandmates?" I asked her in a low voice. "Do I know them, Mom?"

She smiled but her eyes were hiding a certain sadness. "Sometimes, the universe intertwines the paths of two, maybe more, lovely people who lead extravagant lives, only to realize in the end that maybe they weren't meant to cross paths ever again." She rested her chin on the palm of her hand as my shoulders slowly sagged.

"Oh..."

"I'm not saying you aren't meant to meet your friends ever again, but I was talking about me. I'm not meant to meet my friends ever again. The last train had departed and I was too stubborn to realize it."

Mom stared intently at my face, pushing a stray lock of hair behind my ear. Her hand trailed down my face to pinch my chin. I took the chance to cup her face.

"The past is inevitable," I spewed some poetic shit as I stared at her eyes, feeling a lot older than my 15 years. "A scar on our souls reminds us that we got hurt before, but time has healed it. We can't be caged forever by our past. We carry on. We have to."

I thought I made sense but we broke into soft giggles anyway. Mom nodded.

"Your friends are waiting for you, Lu," her eyes sparkled like the Bayanihan sky that Dani and I slept under. "They need you as much as you need them."

She stroked my face one last time with her thumb before letting me go. I stood up slowly on my feet, stretching and feeling rejuvenated. I was a brand new Lu. A Lu who will wow the world. I made one step toward the door, but stopped in my tracks. I forgot something.

Quickly, I turned around and pulled my mom into a tight embrace. She wrapped her arms around me, and we swayed wrapped in each other's arms for a few seconds. She rested her head on my shoulder, and I did the same. Her scent was light and comforting.

"Never commit the same mistake I made, anak," she whispered. "Please do not end up miserable like me." I kissed her on the forehead and on her cheek.

"I know," I said. We stared at each other with smiles stuck on our faces. "Are you alright now?"

"I'm more than alright," she smiled. "I have my barkada, too. And I got to talk to you after a long time. I am fine."

"I'll go for a walk," I grinned as I stepped back, waving goodbye.

"Come back before 6pm."

I rushed to my room to grab my bag and phone. My lock screen was a photo of Alex, Maya, Sachiko, Emmie, and myself on our last day of eighth grade. Along with a cold bottle of water and a wallet with 100 pesos, the mission to retrieve my friends commenced.

26

"Salamat, Ate!" I paid for a pack of Nagaraya, something to munch on while carrying out my mission. The little snack shop was near the park and the clubhouse. Just as I was about to open the pack, my ears caught a guitar solo in the distance. From the clubhouse.

Stuffing the Nagaraya into the bag, I crept up toward the entrance. The melody would start and go on smoothly until a chord would sound out of tune, then there would be a pause before the melody would start all over again. I knocked on the door, but the melody did not stop. So, I decided to slightly open the door and saw a girl against the wall. Alex.

The melody stopped abruptly, like she found a mistake, not in the chords, but something in front of her. She did not bother to offer a smile, or any sign of a warm welcome. But she slid an extra guitar to me. The guitar was bright white, with flowers and butterflies. I crouched down to pick it up, awkwardly positioning myself on the floor.

Alex started to play basic chords. She gave me a side-eye. I knew she was saying, "Well? You aren't gonna harmonize with me?"

I quickly positioned my fingers and began to pluck the strings. The guitar purred proudly.

Bahay kubo
Kahit munti
Ang halaman doon ay sari-sari
Singkamas at talong
Sigarilyas at mani
Sitaw, bataw, patani—

"Let's wrap it up," Alex finally spoke. I followed her directions and we did the last four strums before calling it a day. We smiled and nodded at ourselves before falling into silence again.

"2-x divided by x-squared plus 4x plus 12," Alex threw a random math problem at me.

Silence for a few seconds.

"1 over x +6," I replied softly. She turned to me, this time with a smile on her face.

"So, you did get your brain cells back?" I laughed it off, focusing on the designed guitar she handed me. "This looks so cool."

"Yeah, Maya made it."

I widened my eyes in disbelief, "Shut up."

Alex nodded. I gave out a deep sigh, pursing my lips as I gave another look at the guitar.

"I messed up, Alex…" I mumbled my apology. "I'm sorry I got ma—"

I looked up and caught Alex standing up, hand in the air. Immediately, I crossed my arms over my face, closing my eyes tight. To my surprise, I felt Alex's hand on my cheek.

"Let's get the members back," was all she said.

I smiled with relief. I was back with Alex.

"Man…" Alex looked bummed out. "It's getting late."

"Want to sleep over at my place?" I asked, quite hopeful that she will nod her head.

"Lemme text my mom first."

♪♪

"So, what happened to you guys when I left?" I asked Alex before dropping a spoonful of nilaga and rice inside my mouth.

"Well, not to hurt you but we kind of made a deal with each other not to tell you of our whereabouts. For the main reason that you'd probably get pissed." She wiped her mouth with the pale green napkin.

"Oh." That hurt my appetite so I stopped eating.

"But that was only because Maya feared you'd still be angry," Alex pushed a glass of cold water toward me. "I told her I would visit the clubhouse every day until you come back. I kinda thought if you were 'mad' mad, you wouldn't want to step foot into that place ever again, you know? Now drink some water."

I felt embarrassed, "Oh. Thanks, but I don't wan—"

"Drink."

I let out a small sigh then took a big gulp of cold water. "Well, thanks for believing in me."

"You're like Luka in a way," Alex fed herself some pechay from the nilaga. "You guys get mad really easily, but you calm down when you're given time alone."

"I'm a month older than you."

"A few weeks older than me," Alex clarified. "But you still act like any younger brother. So childish."

We continued stuffing ourselves in between laughter. I missed this.

"Girls, would you like some milk?" Mom asked from the kitchen.

"Yeah," she took her last spoonful of soup, "hopefully it'll help me grow taller than Ems."

I laughed at her comment. The two were pretty much notorious for bickering about their heights, and almost anything under the sun. I guess that was one way to grow closer to each other.

I grabbed our plates and brought them back to the kitchen. I came back with our glasses of milk.

"Let's drink in the cool room," I pointed to the room separated by glass sliding doors at the far end of our house. Alex nodded as she hauled over her backpack and grabbed her glass before making our way to the cool room.

Guests would stay in the cool room since Mom did not like them to go upstairs. Of course, there were exceptions such as Syd's close friends who would hang out in his room. Otherwise, everyone stayed in the cool room where there was a television on one wall, a great view of the backyard, and two huge, reclining couches. Alex and I decided to stay the night in the cool room.

"Claim your spot!" I opened the sliding door.

"Dibs," she placed her bag on the couch covered under a bright pink wool blanket with polka dots and a mustard yellow pillow. I had no choice but to relax on the other couch with a light blue blanket and baby pink pillow.

"May I take a shower first before we discuss anything?" Alex unzipped her backpack to reveal a pair of butterfly pajamas that looked similar to Yukari's.

♪♪

Brrrrrring! Brrrrrrring! We were calling 'The Kid Who'll Metaphorically Hit Me with A Chair.' It was a long name.

"How do you remember everyone with these names?"

"I just do," Alex kept her eyes on the phone, putting it on speaker mode. Then the ringing stopped. We held our breaths.

"Hello?" Sachiko answered.

"Uy, when are you coming back to Manila?" Alex tried to sound like she was alone, just casually calling Sachiko.

"Uh, tomorrow. At like 2pm," Sachiko replied. "Why?"

"I'll visit you."

"Really?!" Sachiko's voice raised with excitement.

"Yeah, I'll even bring a special someone along," Alex hinted.

"Who?!"

"Someone."

"Not fair!"

"Just wait until tomorrow," Alex laughed. "Anyway, see ya, Sach."

"Byeeee." I could sense Sachiko's excitement.

♪♪

I stayed close to Alex despite the absence of a crowd in the airport. Mom waited in the small parking lot.

"They should be coming out now," Alex checked her watch.

Soon after, a crowd of people poured out of the gates. Families, business people, couples, all kinds of people. I could have sworn I saw a dog or two in their small portable cages.

Then we saw a girl our age in a plain black romper walking beside a woman in a black flowy dress, both were wearing shades. The girl was a miniature version of the woman. Wrapped around the girl's arms was a stuffed bunny, her hand holding a phone with a bunny case.

"That can't be Sachiko," I whispered to Alex.

"Oh, yeah, Sach told me about her mom," Alex turned to me. "She's got quite a following in Japan as a fashion designer." Damn.

Sachiko's mom saw us first, but did not say anything to give our presence away. Instead, she whispered something to Sachiko before walking the other way with someone who looked like their chauffeur. Sachiko then walked toward the metal fence and stood there as if waiting for someone.

I almost stopped breathing. She was so close to us, yet she did not notice us.

Her eyes were glued onto her phone. It was a miracle she had not bumped into anyone. She stood right next to Alex. I could tell by Alex's wide eyes that she, too, was surprised at how oblivious Sachiko was. I tried to peek from behind Alex in hopes I could have a better look at Sachiko, but Alex urged me to not reveal myself. Instead, I placed my hands on her shoulders and used all my strength to tiptoe.

We saw a bit of Sachiko's phone screen. Alex's profile icon was on, we tensed up thinking she was about to call Alex. I released my heels and stood flat on the ground before covering my eyes and ears, nervous as to what would happen next.

Alex's phone starts buzzing from the pocket of her hoodie, surprising Sachiko who then turned to see who was next to her. Immediately, a smile adorned her face.

"I was just about to call you!" Sachiko could not contain her happiness as she hugged Alex behind the fence.

"You really took a while to see me," Alex rested her head on Sachiko's shoulder.

I took a step back to watch the two have their moment. Accidentally, I locked eyes with Sachiko, who was surprised judging from the way she widened her eyes and r aised her brows. She released Alex from the hug, went around the fence, and slowly walked toward me. I looked at Alex, a bit worried. She pointed her head toward Sachiko. I took a deep breath.

"Hey, Sach. I wanted to tell you — hopefully, I say this right — gomenasai? Ah, that's probably not right."

Sachiko brought me into a tight embrace. Hesitantly, I patted her back while Alex did a thumbs-up sign and proudly smiled at me. I formed a small smile on my face too.

"One word can heal all troubles," Sachiko said. She pulled back. "How did you know about gomenasai?"

I shrugged, "Ahhh, I made some Japanese friends back at camp."

I mumbled my appreciation for Yukari and Sayaka. They did not only give me tickets to their rookie show, they also gave me a little letter.

Lu!

Since you did not really care about Sachiko and where she came from, here is how to say sorry in Japanese (and other phrases you can use!).

Please use them wisely!

S&Y

"I'm glad you're back," Sachiko smiled.

"I'm even happier that you're back."

There were a lot of questions I wanted to ask Sachiko so I decided start with her trip, "How was Tokyo? And meeting your Star Beats idols? Did you get any tips for playing the keyboard?"

Suddenly, Sachiko's smile faded and she appeared uneasy. She quickly turned to Alex.

"She won't bite, man," Alex explained. "Just tell

her."

Sachiko kept her head down as she spoke, "Well, I might have considered using the synthesizer instead of a keyboard?" She peaked at me, raising her head and squinting her eyes to wait for my response.

"Shut up!" I told her. She looked at me, quite taken aback. Even Alex was nervous as to where this conversation was going.

Quickly, I grabbed both Sachiko's shoulders and shook her gently, "Shut up! Sachiko that's freaking genius! I was actually thinking we could do some kind of transformation to our team."

Sachiko laughed with contained glee while Alex opened her mouth in disbelief.

"Did Tita Mads bring back the right person?" She lightly tapped my cheek.

"I said I was thinking," I raised my hands to show them I was ready for some changes.

"You changed, Lu," Sachiko said.

"She did," confirmed Alex.

Immediately, I placed a finger on my lips and hushed them, "Don't tell anyone though. I'm supposed to be the grumpy one. Don't ruin it for me!"

"Your secret is safe with us," Sachiko promised, giggling while doing so.

"Sachiko!" Sachiko's mom was waving at her and smiling at us. Pretty soul, just like her daughter.

"See you at school, ladies!" Alex and I grinned at the

way Sachiko called us. We watched her run to her mom as Alex announced, "Two more girls."

"Thanks Alex," I genuinely thanked her.

"Save the thanks when all five of us are together," she ruffled my hair. "Anyway, I gotta go. My dad's actually arriving from Singapore in a bit. See ya, Chibi!"

♪♪

"How many more girls to apologize to?" Mom asked as I closed the car door. A soft smile on her face could not comfort the butterflies in my stomach.

"Two. Emmie and Maya."

I was bothered thinking about the them. They were together the longest, and when you make one mad, you make the other furious. It would cost me both my eyes and an arm, or two, to get them to forgive me. Thinking about their angry faces made my stomach twist.

"Maybe you should ask someone for help," Mom hinted.

I remained silent. Asking for help was not easy for me. I needed a push to ask for help. Suddenly, I felt the corner of mom's phone hit my arm. I looked at her, confused.

"Go to Viber. Look for Tita Jaymie's chat." I clicked on Tita Jaymie's profile icon of Emmie and her twin brothers Dominic and Domingo.

"Hi, Jaymie." Mom is a sweetheart, but still a busybody. "Di ba Emmie has a volleyball game next Saturday? Where can I buy tickets for me and Lu?"

Tita Jaymie replied thirty minutes later, "Mads!

Sorry ha for the late reply, but it's free! Just go to Academia de Ascendencia before 2pm to get good seats. I won't tell Emmie that Lu is coming. Baka she'll get distracted. Hahaha!"

Silence. I could not believe that Mom or Tita Mads could be so delightfully charming.

"What do you say, anak?" Mom opened her palm to get the phone back. I placed the phone gently on her palm.

"Thank you, Mom. I owe you a lot!"

27

I was in awe at how spacious Ascendencia's gym was, and how there were actually seats for the audience who were watching the game.

"Mads!" Tita Jaymie waved at us from the front row of the bleachers. Mom patted my back so I could greet Tita Jaymie.

"Thank you for not telling Emmie that I'm here," I told her as my cheek touched her cheek.

"Dapat you tell her, di ba?" Tita Mads' smile was encouraging and sweet. I nodded before making myself comfortable next to Mom.

One of the coaches had asked for a time out by the time I sat down. I looked around and spotted someone familiar from the Ascendencia team, a curvy girl wearing jersey number 20 whose face was flushed red. She was listening attentively to the coach who was probably dictating their next moves. I tried to recall where I had last seen her. I scanned the other seats and spotted a group of girls on their phones while chatting with each other.

Then I heard Dani's laugh.

I sat up straight and my attention went back to the red-faced girl who was probably the team's libero judging from her position at the back of the court. She was the drummer of Timestarterz. A sigh escaped my mouth, relieved that I solved the mystery.

Going back to Emmie and her team, I was surprised that they were doing really well. Emmie had the advantage of being one of the tallest freshmen from St. Teresa's Academy so she strode across the court with ease. Her receives looked so easy and her spikes had the right amount of control and accuracy whenever she hit the ball. The other team would freeze whenever she would spike the ball and would just watch it slam in the space between them, causing a loud roar from those who were cheering for Emmie's team, our school's team.

Even with all her athletic skills though, there was a small detail that caught my eye — Emmie's fingers as she watched the ball arch from court to court. The pointer and middle finger of her right hand were wiggling rhythmically, slightly scratching the side of her thigh.

"Pssst, Lu," someone whispered from behind. I turned quickly to see Sachiko and Alex. Mom scooted two seats away from me. "Girls! You can sit here."

"Thank you, Tita!" Alex thanked her. She went down to the second row of bleachers to sit next to me while Sachiko went all the way down to the front row and awkwardly squeezed her way to sit beside Alex.

"What are you guys doing here?" I whispered.

"To watch Emmie play," Alex raised her brows. "Duh."

"We came here late," Sachiko leaned forward so she could see me. "Did anything happen yet?"

"None, but I learned that this is the school Timestarterz are from," I proudly told them. "Hey, do you notice Emmie's fingers?"

"Ah, yeah," Sachiko nodded. "She's been doing that ever since we disbanded."

"We didn't disband," I corrected her, a bit offended. "We just took a break."

But Emmie's fingers have been wiggling nonstop after our fight? Something about this discovery gave me all the reason to apologize to her. It was my fault.

"Prrrrtttt!" The referee blew the whistle and everyone stood in positive frenzy as our team won against Ascendencia. We made our way out of the bleachers to get to Emmie. On my way up the stairs, I stopped in front of Dani and the keyboardist of Timestarterz, who spotted me first. She then motioned to Dani. Her face lit up to see me.

"I thought I would see you at the battle of the bands!" She was so surprised.

"I don't have time to chat but—" I noticed her phone and its sun and moon-themed case. "You have a new phone. And a new number?" It was a more of a declaration than a question.

Dani looked down at her phone, "Y–yeah. Why?"

I held up my phone with a smirk, "So, what's your new number?" Damn if she's going to brush me off by changing her number.

♪♪

I caught up with Mom, Sachiko, and Alex. Tita Jaymie was with them, too, waiting for the volleyball team of St. Teresa to come out of their dugout. They all ran happily toward Tita Jaymie, screaming joyfully at their victory.

"Okay, girls, wait! Picture! Picture!" Tita Jaymie positioned her phone as the volleyball team huddled together with big smiles plastered on their faces. They started chatting with each other. Alex, Sachiko, and I slowly approached the volleyball team. Emmie spotted us immediately and slowly walked to meet us halfway. She had her poker face on as she towered over us.

"I didn't know you guys came to watch," she sounded quite relieved but her face seemed too tired to show it.

I took one step forward and looked her in the eye, "Um...Emmie, before anything, I just want to say—"

"Ems! There you are!" Pat wrapped her arm around Emmie. "What are you having at Sweet Picnic Lunchroom?" She looked straight into my eyes as she asked Emmie and announced where their team would celebrate their win. "You guys should eat somewhere else."

Alex raised her brows, "Definitely. We're having steak rice. Courtesy of Tita Mads."

"We are?" Sachiko elbowed Alex.

Pat scoffed at Alex. "Emmie here is done with whatever band crap you're involved with. Besides, I think lunchbox cakes would please her more than steak rice."

"That's probably a good point," I agreed, considering how Emmie was into sweets because of Maya's baking phase back in eighth grade.

I stared at Pat, stood my full height, and spoke with as much confidence I could muster, "But I know when Emmie isn't playing volleyball, her fingers become restless and resort to plucking imaginary bass strings."

Talking to Pat scared the living shit out of me. She was not only powerful on the court, but also a very charismatic leader who would not take no for an answer. Plus, she was Aerol tall. But I had to say something to win back Emmie.

I turned to Emmie and pleaded, "I saw how wild your fingers got—would get—when you're stationary. I also know that maybe everything I'm saying is probably wrong and you really like playing volleyball... but I just want you to know that I was a real shithead back then and I'm sorry for being a freaking loser. Okay, I think that's it. I'll just stoptalkingyeahhavefunatthepicniccafething—"

I mumbled the rest as I stepped back and hid behind Alex. Pat was probably going to have a blast poking fun at me.

"Well, Ems?" Pat ignored everything I said.

"Mom!" Emmie shouted to get Tita Jaymie's attention. "I'm eating at Lu's na lang!"

Our jaws dropped when Emmie chose us over her volleyball team.

Tita Jaymie's eyes widened.

"Jay," Mom patted Tita Jaymie's shoulder.

Alex, Sachiko, and I were in pure shock, happy but shocked, and feeling victorious as Pat sourly rolled her eyes at us. Emmie finally formed a small smile on her face.

Without thinking, we hugged each other tight until Emmie stopped us. "I'm sweaty!" We did fist bumps instead.

"Emmie, you can shower in our house if that's okay with you," Mom suggested. Emmie nodded as she hauled her duffel bag over her shoulder.

"What do you want to eat?" I asked.

"I thought you said we'd have steak rice," she looked a bit disappointed. I turned to Mom, who shook her head with a smile, laughing at my stupidity.

"We were actually supposed to have steak rice for merienda," Mom informed us.

♪♪

"It's awfully quiet," Mom laughed at us. Flustered, I tried to initiate a conversation.

"So, um...ho–how's everyone?"

"Good," replied Alex.

"Good," replied Sachiko.

Emmie just had another spoonful of steak rice.

Mom asked, "Is something wrong? Parang whenever I see you together, you're always noisy."

We all nervously laughed before falling silent again.

"It's because Maya's the one who usually starts the conversation," I answered.

Saying Maya's name slowly dampened my appetite as well as everyone else's. It did not feel right eating steak rice without her.

"Has she talked to any of you while I was gone?" I asked.

"She avoided me throughout," Alex answered.

"No texts from her," Sachiko separated the steak and only ate the rice. "I was seenzoned."

Emmie shook her head as she snatched the steak bits from Sachiko's plate.

"Wanna try calling her now?" I suggested. No one replied.

"How about you try calling her?" Alex suggested, receiving nods from Sachiko and Emmie.

I gulped, "O–okay." I grabbed my phone and pressed Maya's number. The phone started ringing.

"The subscriber cannot be reach—"

I turned off my phone. The three looked at me.

"Try again," said Sachiko. I called again.

"The subscriber cannot be reach—"

I called the third time.

"Hello?" It wasn't Maya.

"Mika?" I asked.

"Yeah?"

"Uh...can you get your sister to—"

There was indistinct mumbling at the back on Mika's side.

"Atchi says you can't talk to her." Mika was repeating instructions.

"Oh."

She added, "And she says to fudge off."

I sighed. Classic Maya.

"Please, Mika," I pleaded. "Let me talk to Maya."

"No, you're a bully."

"Okay, I acknowledge that. But if Maya doesn't want to talk through the phone, can I at least talk to her face to face?" There was fumbling.

"Go to the music room after class," Maya's voice was unemotional. "Or get a new drummer." She then hung up.

28

Maya's words played over and over in my head. "Go to the music room after class. Or get a new drummer." We did not want any drummer. Just Maya. How could she even think we would want to replace her?

My eyes focused on the back of her head. She did not even bother to turn her face or body whenever she chatted with our classmate Nina beside her. She had her back turned to me the whole day. Giving up, I turned to Sachiko, who was too focused on her game to care if Maya looked at her or not. I pursed my lips, lowering my head. The moths in my stomach fluttered everywhere too damn much.

Please, God. At least one glance. I don't want Maya to hate me.

"Goodbye and thank you, 9A," Ms. Santos stood up to bid us goodbye.

"Goodbye and thank you, Ms. Santos." We already had our backpacks hauled over our shoulders as we said goodbye. But I still kept my eyes on Maya. She still had the same backpack from eighth grade, only it was cleaner and had way more pins.

There was no sign of drum sticks. It was impossible for me to hope she would still have them after what happened back at the clubhouse. Then again, it would never hurt to ask.

She was one of the first to leave the classroom. I squeezed my way through the narrow gaps between the chairs to catch up with her.

"Maya—" Her name managed to escape my mouth before Alex yanked the straps of my backpack. Emmie was with her.

"Know this about Maya," Emmie placed her hands on my shoulders. "You shouldn't ask her how she's feeling if she's mad at you. What you see is what you get."

She was right.

"Let's all go together," Alex patted Emmie's shoulder. "Baka she's prepping up something in the music room."

We rushed to the fourth floor, anxious of what was going to happen. But the music room was dark from the outside.

"Are we allowed inside?" Sachiko whispered. Alex shrugged.

We threw our bags near the door and stepped inside. Alex bravely walked to the center of the room. The three of us followed, huddling close as we examined the three curved chairs, the keyboards, and the drums in the middle.

Then Maya turned the lights on. I could have sworn she looked different after two weeks.

"Bangs." Emmie pointed out her new hairdo.

"Like 'em?" Maya lightly patted them with her fingertips.

"Yeah," Alex answered. "You look pretty in them."

Maya was delighted at the compliment that she gave her sweetest smile to Alex. But in a second, she went serious.

"Alright, let's cut to the chase," Maya walked closer to us. "So, who wants to guess why we're in the music room?"

"Because we're a band?" Alex guessed.

"Nope."

"Because it's the only room you could reserve!" Sachiko exclaimed.

"Partially correct, but nope."

"Is it because all our instruments are here?" Emmie was sure her guess could be correct.

"Mmm, nope. Seriously, do none of you know?" Maya looked exasperated as she rolled her eyes. I sympathized with her because I knew the answer.

I finally spoke, "How do you not remember? This was where we agreed to become a band."

"Ding ding ding!" Maya clapped her hands, excitement written all over her face. "The reason why I brought you all here was so we could start our quest to rebrand!"

Everyone was silent at her words, all eyes turned to me.

"Guys, I want to play. I missed all of you! But I don't want to play as Syd's Band 2.0. I want to play as us. This sounds cheesy, 'no?" Maya looked at everyone before continuing her monologue. "I thought, we gotta change everything. The band name, the band concept, make it more us, you know? That's why we all chose to be a band.

We chose to play together. So, to start anew, we're going back in time. Take a little trip down memory lane."

Everyone nodded or hummed in agreement. Everyone but me. I stared at her, not nodding at her words, just looking at her. Maya's shoulders sagged when we locked eyes.

"It's just a suggestion," she sounded like she lost hope at having the girls back together and playing as a new band.

"I know," I told her, my eyes softening. "I was wondering when we'll start." They all turned to me as if I was saying gibberish.

"Maya, you're the only drummer I want. And I, too, have been thinking about it. I just didn't know where and how to start."

"Well," her smile was slowly forming, "We can start here. Now."

Like a soldier, she bellowed, "Alright everyone! Grab an instrument!"

I looked around and to my surprise, I saw two guitars and a bass resting on the guitar stands.

"I asked the band club if we could borrow their instruments quickly," Maya explained as she pulled out the drumsticks from inside her backpack.

We grabbed our instruments and began tuning them. Sachiko did a few finger exercises on the keyboard. Alex and I plucked each string to check if our guitars were tuned. Maya hit her foot down on the pedal to hit the bass drum, and Emmie did a quick warm up on the bass.

"Lu? You wanna start us off?" Alex asked. I looked at everyone to make sure they were okay with it. They nodded.

"Alright, let's go with one of the first songs we played," I grinned as I positioned my finger on the C chord.

Alex knew immediately what I would play, "I knew it."

Maya laughed as I got going on this familiar melody. Alex started to pluck the melody to the song I was playing. Sachiko joined in with the piano, harmonizing with Alex's plucking. Emmie added a steady beat to our song. Lastly, Maya topped it off with the main beat, giving this familiar tune a brand, new feel.

"I'll go," I signaled everyone that I was about to sing.

Bahay kubo
Kahit munti
Ang halaman doon
Ay sari-sari

♪♪

"Wrap it up! Wrap it up!" Alex excitedly shouted. Everyone was into the whole idea of rapid strumming, tapping on the keys, plucking, and beating the drum before giving three slow beats, then we waited for Maya to hit the drums once more before giving one final strum. At the end of the children's song, we all laughed loudly.

"I can't believe that was the first song we ever played," Sachiko turned the keyboard off.

"So, what's our next step?" Alex asked as she put away her guitar.

"Our next step will be another practice on Friday after school!" Maya surprised us. We all groaned.

"We seriously have to wait until Friday?" said Sachiko. "The pain I'm feeling is ethereal."

"I think you mean unreal," Alex corrected her.

"I don't want to rush anything," Maya was right so I nodded.

"That's true," Alex finally agreed. "See ya Friday after school, guys."

We went our separate ways, wishing it was Friday already.

29

Friday. 3:40 PM.

I was leaning against the wall near the mall entrance, hoping for someone to find me. I was too early, too anxious to meet my friends after class. As if we were not classmates, haha!

Then I saw a tall girl in a red jacket walk toward me.

"Sup, Chibi!" Alex ruffled my hair.

"You know where everyone else is?" I asked her.

"Nah," she replied. "I just got here."

"Relax, they're coming."

Just in time, we spotted Sachiko in fuzzy pink v-neck sweater, black high-waisted shorts, and white sneakers. So fashionable. She looked like she was having difficulty finding us. Once we locked eyes, she dashed straight toward us.

"There you are, guys!" Sachiko sounded relieved seeing us. "Did you forget we agreed to meet up at the Picnic Lunchroom Cafe?"

Alex and I turned to each other, horrified that we forgot. "We did!" Sachiko rolled her eyes and dragged us to the cafe.

The cafe had vibrant, funky colors and shapes all over the wall. It was full of teens about our age. Boy Pablo was blaring inside. We walked to the end of the cafe where Emmie waited for us. Our rectangle table was so low that our chairs were actually bean bags in different colors.

"You guys took so long," Emmie nagged.

"They waited at the entrance," Sachiko told her. We gave Emmie an awkward smile in hopes she would let us go. I sat beside Sachiko and across Alex while Emmie sat at the head of the table.

A waitress gave us the menus while we waited for Maya. When she arrived, she dressed the part. My mouth dropped when I saw her outfit, a black cami top over a pair of high-waisted shorts that emphasized her curvy body. She had these really cute polymer clay earrings that matched her shorts.

"You look so beautiful," I told her. She pouted.

"That means so much Lu, thanks," she told me.

While waiting for our orders, I asked Maya. "So, what's so special about today?"

Maya pulled out her notebook and pen. "Ladies, today is our last day of being known as Maxxed Out." We all looked at each other with pure excitement at the idea of having a new band name.

"Let's list down our ideas," Maya poised her pen.

"May I be in charge of listing everything down?" I slightly raised my hand. She nodded and passed me her notebook and pen.

New Band Names, I wrote.

"The Cool Kids, but switch the K and the C. The Kool Cids," Alex suggested.

"No, I think we should go with something like... Don't Say No!" suggested Sachiko.

"I think we should use something more...grunge," Emmie shrugged.

While I was writing down all the names, I lifted the notebook to fold it. In doing so, a yellow memo pad fell out and landed on my lap. On it was a drawing of purple flower called named wolf's bane.

"Wolf's Bane!" I exclaimed. "That's our name!"

Everyone stopped talking over each other and looked at me. Maya was the first to comment. "Pretty badass. I like it. How about you, guys?"

"I'm good with Wolf's Bane," agreed Sachiko.

"Wolf's Bane it is!" Alex shrieked.

"It has a pretty cool vibe to it," added Emmie.

"Then it's official!" I wrote our new name under the header and presented it to everyone.

Wolf's Bane

Watching everyone smile at the new band name was like a slap to my face. "Why did not we do this earlier?"

"Alright then, Wolf's Bane!" Alex stood up, really giddy all of a sudden, "Bill's on me!"

"Are you crazy, Alex?!" Emmie tried to pull her down, "We agreed to pay for our own food!"

"Nah," Alex disregarded her. "I've got enough cash to cover for all of us."

"Nooooo! I was the one who asked you all to be here," Maya took her wallet out of her sling bag and raced Alex to the cashier behind me. I did not even bother watching the chaos. I could tell by Emmie and Sachiko's expressions that they did not want to get involved.

While Alex and Maya were paying at the cashier, I grabbed a transparent bandage from my pocket and used it as tape, sticking the Wolf's Bane drawing under our brand new name. Satisfaction was written all over our faces as we drank it in.

Done with the payment, I asked the girls, "So, where's our next location, wolves?"

"Are we actually called wolves?" Alex laughed as we exited the cafe.

"I think it sounds cute," Maya said.

"Well, what are we doing next?" I asked again.

"Come."

We all followed Maya as she turned a corner and stopped in front of Salon de Mark.

"This is your Tito Mark's hair salon!" Emmie announced.

"Yes, I get discounts because I'm his favorite niece," Maya winked and pushed the glass doors. We were greeted with the fragrant smell of shampoo and piped-in acoustic music. When the receptionist saw Maya, she rushed to Mark who was working on a middle-aged lady. He asked his assistant to take over before rushing to give Maya a tight embrace.

"My sweet Maya!" Tito Mark happily squealed. When he released Maya, he scanned the rest of us and whispered something to Maya. Once she nodded, he escorted us to the back of the salon.

"Where are we going?" Alex whispered.

"Beats me," Emmie shrugged.

Tito Mark opened a white door to an empty room with five chairs, two hair washing stations, and two carts full of hair supplies.

"This is our creativity room," he said. "This was where Maya gave herself these beautiful bangs."

"Woah!" Sachiko pointed to Maya's bangs, "You did that yourself?" Maya nodded as we entered the room and grabbed seats to examine our own hair.

My hair rested on my shoulders, I did not like it long like Emmie's nor did I want it mid length like Sachiko's and Alex's. But, honestly, I was growing sick of this hair.

"Now, before we do anything," Maya walked like a strict proctor behind our seats, "I did let your moms know I will be changing your hairstyles. We won't do anything hardcore like dying our hair."

"Aw, man," Alex sighed, making us all laugh.

"Although…" Maya picked up a basket of colored hair spray and paraded the loot for everyone to see. We cheered as she placed the basket on the table between me and Alex. Then she pulled out her phone and connected it to the speakers. Upbeat, indie songs began to play out loud, setting the mood.

"So, who's first?" I asked, getting a bit nervous.

"Sachiko?" Maya suggested.

"Uh..." Sachiko stared at the pair of scissors on the table.

"I don't see why you guys are scared of cutting your hair," Alex stood up from her chair and grabbed a pair of scissors and a lock of Sachiko's hair. "It'll just grow out again!"

Snip!

Our mouths fell wide open at the lock of hair that fell gracefully onto the floor. And it was at this very moment that I discovered that Sachiko could hold high notes.

"I'm sorry!" Alex pleaded for forgiveness as Sachiko freaked out and stood up from her chair. Emmie was trying so hard not to laugh, so was Maya.

"Sach! I think you'll look great with short hair!" I tried calming her down. "Less distractions while playing Star Beats."

"In that case," Sachiko sat down, "Alex, can you chop off everything?" We all looked at her, surprised at her request.

"I can't believe she bought that," I said.

"Yo, Maya! Can you do the honors?" Alex handed Maya the scissors. "That was traumatic."

"Alright! Let's wash your hair first!" Maya guided Sachiko to the hair washing station. And just like that, we started our reset session from Maxxed Out to Wolf's Bane.

"Wow," Sachiko puffed up her new short hair. "I feel lightheaded. Is this how Lu feels?"

"Haha! You're right about that!" I watched her enjoy her new look before raising my hand. "May I go next?"

"Let's spray your hair blue," Alex grabbed the spray can. "Because it rhymes with Lu."

"That's such a ridiculous reason."

Psssshhhhhhhh!

"Dude! Give me a warning!" I shrieked as the cold mist from the paint touched my scalp.

Alex did not look satisfied though. "Your hair's so dark the blue spray just made it look oily."

"Lu, do you have any haircut in mind?" Maya asked.

I quickly pulled out my phone and showed her a photo of Syd's last hairstyle before he died. "I may have moved on, but that still doesn't mean I can just simply throw him out of this band thing."

Maya zoomed in on the photo and looked at my hair. She bit her inner cheek. "A challenge, huh? I'm up for it. Let's hope you don't go bald."

Being bald doesn't sound that bad.

"I trust you, Maya, so…" I closed my eyes and put out my hands, palms up. Maya took my left arm and guided me to the hair washing station. Throughout the trimming, my eyes were closed. Thirty minutes after, I opened them when Maya said she was done.

I could not believe what I saw in the mirror.

"Holy shit, she looks like her brother," Alex whispered.

"Yooo!" Sachiko shouted.

"Syd? Is that you?" Emmie asked.

I almost cried. My hair went the whole 180. I was hesitant to touch it because I did not want to mess it up. Instead, I stood up and hugged Maya tightly.

"I totally love it, Maya," I held back my tears of joy.

"I'm glad you do. You look so good with Syd's haircut."

Alex patted my back, "Lu, you really look like Syd. It's scary." She turned to Maya and said, "You did a really great job with Lu's hair."

I was about to take a photo of my hair to send to Mom and Dani when a familiar guitar riff started playing. Then came the lyrics.

> *Take that picture from our frame,*
> *I'll put it in my pocket so that everyday you're with me*
> *I'll keep it close in my heart.*

I looked for the phone.

"Why Lu?" Maya asked.

"It's just—" I pointed to Maya's phone. "This is my jam!"

"You? Liking music from Maya's Magic Stuff? Shut up!" Emmie could not believe me.

"I played this song at camp! Fell in love with it!" I managed to say just in time to scream with the chorus.

> *And we'll be back before you knooooow*
> *You knoooooow it*
> *La la la la la la la la!*

Maya jumped with pure joy as she joined me.

"Aaaaa! I feel accomplished in life!" Maya screamed. "I got to style all of you and I got Lu to like a song from my playlist!"

"You didn't style Alex's," Emmie corrected her.

Alex pointed at Emmie, "Hey, Maya didn't style yours either."

"How about we play a game of rock paper scissors," Emmie taunted. "Loser goes bald."

"Deal!" Alex was just about to start a round before Maya disconnected her phone from the speakers.

"Let's get out of here before anything worse happens," Maya stopped the two from losing their hair. "Besides, it's almost five. I've got one more spot to show you."

We run to the mall's rooftop to witness a perfect view of the city and the sun bidding its farewell for a good day's work. The five of us sat on the concrete floor, soaking all the remaining sunlight in.

"Glad we made it on time," Emmie spoke.

"Lu?" Maya turned to me. "Do you have something to say?"

"Yeah," I smiled as I faced the setting sun. The girls crowded around me.

"That whole week away from each other after the fight taught me a lot about me. I really messed up our friendship by choosing to remain in the past and holding all of us back from growing. I'm sorry for that. But even if I messed up, you guys still stuck by my side, and I think this whole love for being in a band may have seemed like it all started with my brother, but when I think about it, I liked being in a band because it was how I expressed my thankfulness for having people like you. Thanks, guys."

Four pairs of eyes looked at me with understanding and warmth that there was no need for any word. I put out my hand. Alex placed her hand on mine. Sachiko lightly placed hers on top of Alex's. Emmie placed her hand on top of Sachiko's. Maya placed her hand over Emmie's.

I continued, "Let's have fun at the Battle of the Bands. Let's practice hard not for first place, but for us. Let first place just be a bonus. Let's play with our heart and have each other's backs. Wolf's Bane on three. One, two—"

"Can we howl instead?" Alex interrupted.

I shrugged, "Zero complaint against that. One, two, three!"

"Wolf's Bane!"

"Wolf's Bane!"

"Wolf's Bane!"

"Wolf's Bane!"

We exchanged confused looks, expecting Alex to howl. Smiles turned into fits of laughter followed by gentle slaps on Alex's arm.

30

I was the last to enter the clubhouse. "Did you jump out your window again?" Maya asked coldly.

I laughed, "I used the front door this time."

She rubbed my back, "That's great."

"Guys, can we all huddle in the center first?" I asked as I laid my guitar bag next to me on the floor. I brought out the notepad Hachi gave me while waiting for everyone to gather. Then I flipped my notepad to the page with the lyrics I wrote from camp.

"Let's perform something original for the Battle of the Bands," I told them. "Alex? Could you bring your guitar here?"

"Sure," Alex stood up to grab her guitar that rested on the table.

"Remember that melody you played when we met again?"

"I haven't really polished it."

"It's alright, but can you play it?"

Alex started to play the melody she had been practicing, seducing everyone with the haunting sound. After a few seconds of instrumental, I began to add the lyrics to her melody.

Did you know that gravity pulls sideways
We don't have forever to debate
And love is not
Like a game of cards, where
We both are fours, and you need an eight.

"Yooo! That sounds pretty good," Maya clapped her hands.

"You sure?" Alex grabbed the notepad and looked at the words. "I think we tweak the chords a bit to fit Lu's vocals."

"It also sounds pretty incomplete," Emmie added.

I looked at Emmie, "We might need to brainstorm for a second verse, a chorus, and a bridge."

"Maybe we can spend today brainstorming then?" Emmie suggested.

I nodded, "That'd be great."

Just as we were about to start, we heard a knock on the door.

Alex stood up and noticed our confused faces. "Why? If we're gonna be using our brains, we might as well eat something, you know." She walked up and opened the door to reveal Aerol in his pizza uniform.

"Oi!" Sachiko pointed to him. "It's pizza boy!"

"Aerol!" I rushed to the door and just smiled at him while Alex was counting her money.

"Hi, Lu."

To Alex, he said, "That'll be 450 pesos." Alex looked at me automatically.

"Fifty?"

"Yeah, that will do."

As she handed the money to Aerol, he said, "Break a leg at the competition."

"We'll break both our legs," Sachiko shouted from behind, giggling at her response. "And our arms, too, while we're at it!"

Alex and I awkwardly laughed at Sachiko's enthusiasm.

"See ya, Aerol," I smiled.

"Great to see you smile, Lu," he ruffled my hair. "Bye, girls!"

Alex closed the door and rushed to the center with the two boxes of pizza, excited to eat all of them at once.

"Food, pens, instruments," I listed all the materials we'll need. "Right! Let's get creative!"

♪♪

Do you know why—

I scratched the back of my neck as my voice cracked.

Do you—
Do you know why—

"Aagh!"

We had been practicing for a few weeks now. We got the song down and now we were making sure playing it was muscle memory at this point. Since practice was during school, we agreed to meet every

Wednesday (if we had no quiz the next day), Fridays, and Saturdays. Sometimes, we would be lucky enough to spend our lunch time at the music room with Mr. Reyes supervising us.

"The competition's already this Saturday," I caressed my throat. "Why am I only messing up now?"

Mom opened the sliding doors to my room and placed a small cup on my table. "I can hear your groans from my room, anak," she pushed the cup closer to me. "Ginger tea with honey will help."

"Thanks, Mom," I took a sip of the tea, feeling my throat slowly getting soothed by the concoction.

"You're so much like your brother," Mom sighed. "Take a break na. Sige ka, baka you won't have a voice on Saturday." I shuddered at the humiliation that would stick with me if that actually happened. She then patted my hair, "You look so great with this haircut."

"Thanks, mom," I lowered my head, shy to receive a compliment from her. She kissed my head before walking out of my room. Then I remembered Sachiko's mom's reaction when she saw her daughter's new cut. I grabbed my phone and looked for the video from the Wolf's Bane group chat. I clicked on it.

"Mama!" Sachiko called. Her mom entered her room, her eyes widening at the sight of Sachiko's new do. Her mom's mouth slowly curved upward.

"Your cut your hair," her mom touched Sachiko's hair.

"Do you like it?" Sachiko asked.

Her mom nodded as she puffed up Sachiko's hair.

"You look so beautiful, Sachiko!"

I was just about to send a sticker to the group when Dani's name came up. She was calling me.

"Turn on your camera, Lu!" I turned on my camera.

She gasped. "Oh, my gosh."

I smiled at Dani's response. "Hi, Dani."

"You really look like Syd, oh my gosh—"

"I was thinking of surprising you," I frowned. "How did you know I cut my hair?"

"Carla. Apparently, she and Sachiko got close while we were at camp." Dani ate her cheese fries as soon as she got over the shock of seeing my new haircut.

"Ah, that makes sense," I thought back at how Sachiko wanted to start using the synthesizer. "How did they meet ba?"

"Carla attended this event for a game she plays and met Sachiko there."

"Oh, Star Beats!" I exclaimed.

"Yeah, that was the name."

"Tell Carla thanks by the way," I glanced at my guitar that rested next to me. "I think she helped Sachiko come out of her shell."

Dani laughed, "You don't even know how much Carla's been talking about her."

"Oh, how the tables have turned." The two of us laughed softly before quieting down, thinking of what to say next.

"But, omg! You really look like Syd," Dani repeated.

"Do I look good though?" I asked.

"Yeah! You rock it, Lu."

"I do? Well, thank you." I took a sip of the ginger tea.

"Welcome!" Dani laughed before moving onto a more serious question. "Are you ready for this Saturday?"

"Kind of," I massaged my neck. "What about you?"

"I'm nervous."

"Is it your mom?"

"Kind of, but not really. We had a talk about Timestarterz when I got back from camp."

"Oh. Great."

Dani's voice seemed sad as she continued, "Yeah, but I'm more worried about our moms meeting each other. I think they have an unresolved business."

"I really don't know." But I think my mom knew the answer.

"She revealed a lot of things after camp."

"Like what?" She could have seen that same livestream, I thought.

"She told me about Breaking Daylights, how both our moms were there, and this other girl named Cheryl, I think. I've never heard of her, but it seemed that she was someone really important to my mom and Tita Mads. Then she died and our moms got into some heated argument. After that, my mom was determined that I never see you again. That's why I left Maxxed Out. My mom was scared for me." I saw her sigh as she continued. "To be honest, everything I told you that night was a lie."

A sharp pain hit my chest, but I tried to not show any emotion.

"I hated pop, but I left the band because my mom would have been mad if I didn't. It kinda worked in my favor though. It led me to Carla and Martha. Then my mom wanted to send me to some stupid camp to take a break before Battle of the Bands, which was really dumb because I could've used that time to practice."

I nodded furiously.

"But funny enough it led me to you again."

The pain soon faded, replaced by fluffy clouds and butterflies.

"No doubt she wanted Timestarterz to beat whatever band you were in. She knew how passionate you were about music, it scared her. It's freaking weird though. Not even my being at the top of my class made her happy. She seemed determined that Timestarterz beat your band."

I did not understand where her mom was coming from but I could actually relate in a way.

"It made me freaking sick, Lu. She started treating my band as her band. Suddenly, music stopped being fun. It became a chore, another subject at school to stay at the top off or else I'd be nothing."

I felt the pressure on Dani, and I wonder why I did not see that.

"But you know, that performance back at camp has got to be my favorite performance ever."

"Oh, it was definitely one of my favorites."

"I think we kicked ass that day." Dani's words lifted the joy level one notch higher that I had to laugh at her excitement.

"You think so?" My heart was fluttering as I asked her.

"Wait, you don't think so?"

"Of course, I think so!"

I leaned back and remembered Aerol's words. "I think Aerol's right, Dani. We do not need to be in the same band. We're better off like this."

"Yah. But I just do not know how our moms would behave should they see each other this Saturday."

"Shouldn't that be their problem and not ours?" Dani nodded and went silent for a second or two.

"Lu, I have zero clue what their fight was about, or how Tita Cheryl died, but that shouldn't mean we have to carry on as if their issues are our issues. Right? I just want my mom to see you as Lu and not as Tita Mad's daughter, you know?"

"True, I wish they make up though." We nodded at the same time.

"Anyway, what song are you gonna perform?" Dani asked casually.

"Dude, that's cheating!"

"Fine," Dani gave up. But she continued, "I'm nervous about performing."

"Me, too," I opened up. "Like, what if my voice stops?"

"Dude, same!" Dani lit up.

"I hope your voice doesn't dry out."

"I hope yours doesn't as well."

"I'll go practice a bit more."

"Okay."

"See ya, Dan."

"See ya."

We hung up. I meant to send a cheesy message to her. Then Dani sent me a photo of a cat screaming and surrounded by heart emojis of different colors. I smiled and sent her a sticker of two bunnies hugging.

Placing my phone down, I picked up my guitar and continued where I left. Closing my eyes, I chanted silently in my head. Please don't break. Please don't break.

I focused on my fingers and how they were positioned on each string, adding pressure if a chord did not sound right. Nervous to crack my voice for the nth time, I mumbled the lyrics.

Did you know that gravity pulls sideways

I watched my fingers switch chords on time.

We don't have forever to debate
And love is not like a game of cards
Where we are both fours, and you need an eight

I gave one last strong strum as I stared at the wall in front of me. Satisfied, I nodded and placed my guitar down on the guitar stand.

"Calling it a day," I told myself as I stretched out on the bed, finding a comfortable position so as to be fully relaxed. Then a notification from Sachiko came in.

"Lu! Check it out!" There was an image of a synthesizer. "Mom surprised me with one! It's a game changer!"

31

Sachiko was right. The synthesizer was a game changer. She tried it out by playing Bahay Kubo and Reptilia, and it gave the songs brand new vibes.

"Just imagine what this could do to our new song," Sachiko said, confessing her love for her new instrument while the rest of us sat on monobloc chairs. Good decision to let her play it because she wanted to, I thought to myself.

Maya turned to me, "What's the title of our song?"

Oh, my goodness. "Shit, how did I forget that?" I pinched the bridge of my nose in disappointment. I was too deep in the lyrics that I did not think of a suitable title.

"Don't you want to call it Wolf's Bane?" Emmie suggested.

"Sounds like a PowerPoint presentation," Alex shook her head. "Think of something more connected to the lyrics."

"Purple hearts!" Maya shouted as if her life depended on it.

"Genius!" I shouted back, giving her a high five.

"Purple Hearts by Wolf's Bane," Alex repeated the title. "Got a nice ring to it."

"You know what else would give it a nice ring?" Sachiko pointed to the synthesizer, "If we could play the song with the synths."

I stood up and walked to my guitar, "What Sachiko wants, she gets."

"Aight," Alex stood up from the chairs and jogged to her guitar. Maya and Emmie walked up to their respective instruments.

"Maya, give us the signal," I adjusted the strap on my shoulder. I liked wearing my guitar around my midsection because my limbs weren't long enough to let the guitar hang low, unlike Emmie's or Alex's. Maya held the sticks up to the air and banged them thrice. "One! Two! Three!"

Taking notes from how Timestarterz performed their instrumentals, we moved our bodies to channel our energy to the audience before the first verse. Alex hopped a lot on her feet, even turning around once in a while to play with Sachiko. I have seen Alex several times leaning forward into her guitar, cradling and comforting it, almost touching the floor, whenever she was into a song.

Emmie would look at both the audience and at her bass before moving her fingers to the next chord. She would sway back and forth to calm herself, disguising her stage fright.

Maya the drummer could not move around a lot, so she showed various expressions while playing. We would make eye contact while playing then share a giggle or two.

I moved forward to start singing as I placed both my hands on the microphone.

The synthesizers gave Purple Hearts the vibes it definitely needed. This new sound really reflected what Wolf's Bane aspired to be. A band not created because Lu misses her brother, but a band created because five girls wanted to play music together.

It was time to sing the chorus and focus on Sachiko. She either bobbed her head side to side or concentrated on the keys with such tenacity she seemed lost in her own world. We made eye contact though and she grinned as she turned away to plunge some keys. I looked down at my hands as they switched from one chord to the next as the song continued.

One of the best feelings about playing together would definitely be that last strum before the song officially ends. We would all turn around to face Maya as she led the final seconds that built up to one loud explosion of all five instruments.

"And that's a wrap!" I gave everyone a high five.

"Gahhh," Emmie did a facepalm. "I totally messed up the chorus."

"Oh, my gosh! Me, too," Sachiko pointed to herself.

I shrugged, "You guys gotta put your head in the game then. Besides, this'll be our last practice before the competition." I placed my guitar back in its case, "We'll rest a day before the competition. We've been going at this for almost five weeks already."

"But I'm not ready to leave you guys after so long," Maya dramatically back hugged Emmie out of sadness.

"Come on," I patted Maya's back. "We all did so well the past few weeks. We all deserve a rest."

Sachiko turned to Maya as she placed the synthesizer in its own case, "You can come over to my house to help me and my mom pick out the stage outfits."

"Really?!" Maya's sad face immediately brightened up at the thought of visiting Sachiko's place.

"Dude, that's a pretty huge achievement," Alex hauled her guitar bag over her shoulder. "First person to visit Sachiko's house? You deserve a medal."

"Alright," I scanned the practice room. "Did anyone forget anything? Maya, how are you bringing home the drums?"

"I read the venue will provide us with one," Maya placed her drum sticks inside her backpack.

"Alright! Out, everyone!"

"Rest well!" Alex opened the door and disappeared.

"Ahhh, I'm excited!" Sachiko followed.

"Maya, you need help?" Emmie waited for Maya. I walked ahead of them.

"Bye, everyone!" I waved at the last car to leave the village as I turned to walk back home. Mom waited on a bench at the corner of the park.

"Mom!" I rushed to her and gave her a tight squeeze. "Why are you here?"

"Sit here, anak," she scooted a bit so I could sit next to her. I noticed she was holding a pick with a crescent moon drawn on it. I took it from her hand, examined it closer, and flipped to read Luna on one side.

"That was my stage name when I performed with the girls," Mom reminisced. "And that was the pick that helped me write the first song Syd learned on the guitar."

"For me?" I could not believe it.

"I already sucked up all the luck it could give me," Mom laughed. "Seemed like it wanted a new owner."

I stared at the name. Luna.

32

Sancta Caecilia was one of the best art schools in Manila. Their stadium has a huge stage and almost a thousand seats. There was a second floor with even more seats. I doubted that would get filled, but it would be pretty wild if it did.

"Uy! Lu!" I saw Tita Jaymie rush from backstage. "Hurry up! Everyone's waiting for you!"

In the waiting area, Sachiko's mom waited. When she saw me, she closed her phone and stood up immediately.

"Lu! Your clothes!" She handed me a top and a bottom as well as a pair of shoes. "Go to the dressing room."

"The other girls are there changing pa," Tita Jaymie told me.

I rushed to the dressing room and spotted Maya putting on lip gloss.

She rushed to hug me. "Hurry up and change already!" She wore a loosely fitted striped collar tee with high-waisted denim shorts and a pair of Doc Martens.

Alex appeared in a black striped t-shirt that was slightly fitted and her black pants had loose straps hanging on each side of her legs. She wore a pair of white sneakers. "This stall's open."

"Gotcha," I entered the stall and unfolded the clothes Sachiko and Maya assigned to me. I got a dark purple hoodie that exposed my right shoulder, a pair of black sweats, and black rubber shoes. The clothes felt so comfortable that I could wear them the whole day.

Sachiko saw me first when I got out of the stall, "Nice shoulder you got there, Lu." She wore something similar to Alex. Black tee, black pants, and white sneakers. The words Road Trip was written across her chest and her black denim pants had frays that rested on her ankles.

Emmie, on the other hand, wore a hooded blue crop top with a sunflower patch on her left breast. It ended just above her distressed high-waisted jeans that covered her black Doc Martens.

"Emmie's our star for this performance," Maya hugged her. We all nodded in agreement.

"Let's head back to the waiting room," Alex rubbed her stomach. "I've been eyeing the pizza there since I got here." True enough, she grabbed two slices of the cheese pizza as soon as we got to the waiting room.

It was not long before the doors to our waiting room opened. Dani poked her head in.

"Dani!" I ran to her and gave her a tight hug. Carla, Martha, and Aerol followed behind her.

"May we share waiting rooms?" Aerol politely asked Tita Jaymie.

"Sure!" Tita Jaymie stood up and held the door for them.

Alex stood up, "Guys, let them sit on the couch.

They're wearing skirts." Wolves Bane eyed Timestarterz before quickly standing up and offering the couch to the newcomers.

Dani had her hair styled into two cute space buns. She wore a white t-shirt with a rose in the middle, tucked into a baby pink skirt that stopped halfway at her thighs. Carla wore a white t-shirt with words across her chest, and tucked into a periwinkle skirt with ruffles. She had a blue beret that rounded out her style. Martha wore a cropped turquoise long-sleeved shirt with a French word written in cursive across her chest and a drawing of a lip stain below it, a white high-waisted skirt, and a pink beret that matched Dani's skirt.

"You guys look so cute!" I covered my mouth immediately at the unexpected compliment. Carla nudged Dani, who pushed her back. I watched the girls of Wolf's Bane look at each other in pure confusion.

"Are we missing anything, Lu?" Maya wrapped her arm around me. I faked a smiled at her, then at Timestarterz.

"Nope! Absolutely nothing."

Dani sat on the very right of the couch, nearest to my guitar bag. She pulled it forward so she could have a better look at it. The pudding keychain caught her eye as she held it with her hand.

"You still have Mr. Pudding," she sounded emotional.

"I thought I told you that," I pulled a chair closer to her as I grabbed my guitar bag. Unzipping my guitar, I pulled it out and rested it on my thigh.

"How about a little warm up before we go on stage?" I started playing the first chord of Bahay Kubo, "Ba—"

"Oh my gosh! This is the third time this week, Lu!" Emmie interrupted me. "You really don't have any other song to play?" Sachiko covered her mouth in full shock. Dani covered her mouth, trying to hide her laughter. I knew Emmie was joking, considering how her mouth slowly curved upward as she stifled a laugh.

"Do you not know the importance of this song?" I stood up, "This song unites all of us!" I spread my arms and looked up to the ceiling. "For we are all… vegetables!"

No one laughed at my exclamation.

"Vegetables?" Carla repeated.

"Lu, what time did you sleep last night?" Aerol asked, concerned.

I tried to look annoyed, "We're all vegetables! It's that simple!" I pointed to everyone in the room, "You're a vegetable! You're a vegetable! You're a vegetable! You're a vegetable! You're a vegetable! You're a vegetable! And you're a vegetable! We're all vegetables!"

Slowly, I heard soft giggles from Maya and Martha. Their laughs slowly infected the rest of us. Seeing the whole room laugh at whatever crap I was trying to preach was music to my ears. I lowered my head to rub my forehead.

"Shoot, I lost my train of thought. But wait! What I'm trying to say is that, like the vegetables, we're all different. But we're all united under one Bahay Kubo. Which is?"

"The Philippines?"

Sachiko's innocent answer brought the whole waiting room into fits of laughter. I looked up for divine guidance before I revealed the answer.

"Music! We're all united under music!"

Everyone stopped laughing.

"Ohhhh."

I could bet on Aerol's Pizza that they were all trying to analyze the depth of my vegetable philosophy. Defeated, I collapsed beside Dani, who continued to laugh at my preaching and the way I slouched on the chair. I looked at her, and began to laugh softly.

Then the door opened. A staff looked around first before declaring, "Timestarters, get on the stage in three."

"Break a leg, Dani," I shook her hand.

"Thanks," she squeezed my hand. "You, too." She checked to see if Carla and Martha were ready to go before walking out of the waiting room. Aerol gave me a nod before catching up with them.

A voice roared, "Here comes the first band! From Academia de Ascendencia… Timestarterz!" There was a loud applause and booming cheers that sent chills down my spine.

The same staff member opened the door to our waiting room, "Wolf's Bane, you're next."

Tita Jaymee pointed to the television on one wall, "Girls, they're streaming the acts here." We all huddled in front of the television, excited to see what Timestarterz had in store for us.

The vibrant colors of blue, pink, and purple lights shone on the three girls on the huge stage. The sound of the synthesizer that accompanied Dani's sweet lyrics turned the auditorium into a candy wonderland.

There was something special about this performance. Dani was not the same pastel wannabe I saw at the opening ceremony. I was seeing a self-confident Dani with her genuine smile, perfectly channeling her endearing song.

Carla bopped her head to the beat, pressing her synthesizer that radiated unique Timestarterz sound. Her smile grew wider as her eyes were glued to Dani.

Martha was accurately hitting every beat, keeping a steady tempo as she smiled back at Carla, and looking like a proud mom as Dani danced with her bass.

When they finished, the crowd screamed even louder.

"Ah, gosh! That was so much serotonin," Maya clutched her heart.

"That was so cute," Alex clutched her heart, too, and did a little stumble.

"Guys!" I clapped to get their attention. "We're up next!"

"Go, get 'em, Wolf's Bane!" Tita Jayme and Sachiko's mom cheered us on as we rushed out of the waiting room with our instruments and toward the stairs that lead to the stage.

We could not see the person behind the booming voice but we heard him loud and clear. "Up next is the band from St. Teresa Academy. Raise your hands for... Wolf's Bane!"

We ran up the stage and saw the hyped-up crowd up to the second floor of the stadium. I called everyone to huddle in the center of the stage first.

"We all believed Maxxed Out would never come this far." I tried to control my shaky voice so they would not think I was scared shitless. "We were right, because it was Wolf's Bane that would have made it this far. So, let's show them what we've got, alright?" They nodded.

"Wolves on three. One! Two! Three!" Oddly, we all howled this time.

The crowd was thrilled, igniting our passion to show them what we got. We all rushed to our positions, then Maya banged her sticks, "One! Two! Three! Go!"

We launched Purple Hearts with an instrumental opening, and the crowd liked it. We moved on to the rhythm and they swayed with us. I strutted up to Emmie for a small dance, egged her for a little hop and skip to calm her nerves. She gave me a sweet smile that told me she was okay. I smiled back and ran straight to Alex and Sachiko. We banged our heads to the beat of Maya's drum. I turned to wave at Maya before walking up to the mic for the first verse.

Letting go of my guitar, letting it hang, I gripped the mic, savoring this moment as the screams poured down on us like a waterfall. I sang to the crowd's delight.

Something about the screams was comforting. A continuous momentum that would carry throughout the song. I opened my eyes to look at the crowd. People of different ages cheering us on, but my eyes automatically focused on a specific face. Mom's. She made it!

I totally forgot the weight of the Fender as I took a few steps back.

"Lu!" Maya's voice startled me. I turned to face her as she giggled at my mistake. I fixed my stance, glancing at my shoes before I looked up. I strummed my guitar and took a good look at everyone around me. Emmie, Maya, Sachiko, Alex. I was not alone.

I held the mic with one hand as I waved to the pumped-up crowd, sang our song, and looked at my friends whose smiles were as bright as the spotlights that shone on each of us.

This was my dream.

This was our dream.

Glossary

Anak — child; also an endearment for a younger person

Atchi — eldest sister

Ate — older sister or relative

Ay, naku. — What the heck?

Ano ba yan? — What is that?

Ba't ang bagal? — Why so slow?

Bahay — house

Banig — woven mat

Barkada — a group of friends

Basta — an expression

Bastos — rude

Buhay — life

Dapat — roughly translates to 'should'

Di ba? — Isn't it?

Dibs — colloquial for 'first choice'

Din — also

Galing — Great!

Gulay — vegetables

Ha — 'What?' and also roughly translated to 'okay'

Ikaw talaga — no exact translation; may express any emotion from exasperation to embarrassment to surprise or gratitude; roughly translated to 'Oh, (Name)' (for example: Oh, Sachiko)

Kaldereta — beef stew in tomato sauce

Kuya — older brother

Luh — an expression; shortened form of hala; Oh, no!

Merienda — snack

Na — already

Naman — may express any surprised emotion or disbelief [Sachiko naman!]

Nilaga — a clear, sweet broth made from meat and vegetables

Pala — roughly translated to 'I just realized that…'

Salamat po — Thank you.

Sige na — roughly translated to 'Please.'

Sige ka — roughly translated to 'You better watch out.'

Sino — who

Tama na — Enough!

Tiangge — mom-and-pop store

Tita — auntie

Tito — uncle

Uy — Hey

Uy, bilisan mo! — Hey, hurry up!

www.ingramcontent.com/pod-product-compliance
Lightning Source LLC
LaVergne TN
LVHW041910070526
838199LV00051BA/2564